FEELS LIKE HOME

BY:
BROOKE ST. JAMES

Feels Like Home

Published in Nashville, Tennessee, by Elm Hill, an imprint of Thomas Nelson. Elm Hill and Thomas Nelson are registered trademarks of HarperCollins Christian Publishing, Inc.

Elm Hill titles may be purchased in bulk for educational, business, fund-raising, or sales promotional use. For information, please e-mail SpecialMarkets@ThomasNelson.com.

ISBN 978-1-4003-3693-7

Other titles available from Brooke St. James:

Another Shot:
(A Modern-Day Ruth and Boaz Story)

When Lightning Strikes

Something of a Storm (All in Good Time #1)
Someone Someday (All in Good Time #2)

Finally My Forever (Meant for Me #1)
Finally My Heart's Desire (Meant for Me #2)
Finally My Happy Ending (Meant for Me #3)

Shot by Cupid's Arrow

Dreams of Us

Meet Me in Myrtle Beach (Hunt Family #1)
Kiss Me in Carolina (Hunt Family #2)
California's Calling (Hunt Family #3)
Back to the Beach (Hunt Family #4)
It's About Time (Hunt Family #5)

Loved Bayou (Martin Family #1)
Dear California (Martin Family #2)
My One Regret (Martin Family #3)
Broken and Beautiful (Martin Family #4)
Back to the Bayou (Martin Family #5)

Almost Christmas

JFK to Dublin (Shower & Shelter Artist Collective #1)
Not Your Average Joe (Shower & Shelter Artist Collective #2)
So Much for Boundaries (Shower & Shelter Artist Collective #3)
Suddenly Starstruck (Shower & Shelter Artist Collective #4)
Love Stung (Shower & Shelter Artist Collective #5)
My American Angel (Shower & Shelter Artist Collective #6)

Summer of '65 (Bishop Family #1)
Jesse's Girl (Bishop Family #2)
Maybe Memphis (Bishop Family #3)
So Happy Together (Bishop Family #4)
My Little Gypsy (Bishop Family #5)
Malibu by Moonlight (Bishop Family #6)
The Harder They Fall (Bishop Family #7)
Come Friday (Bishop Family #8)
Something Lovely (Bishop Family #9)

CHAPTER 1

Spring, 1994

Evan King
(Daniel & Abby's youngest son)

*E*van was near the end of his junior year of college. He was a star running back for the University of Nebraska Cornhuskers football team, and they were just coming off an amazing season. They won the conference championship this year, but they lost a heartbreakingly close game against Florida State in the Orange Bowl. That was a couple of months ago, and Evan's life was quieter now that the season had ended.

After the bowl game, Evan went back to Nebraska to finish his semester at school. He lived in Lincoln full-time now. When he was a freshman, he went home to Galveston any chance he got, but his life had gotten busier as the years passed, and now he stayed in Nebraska during breaks and relied on his parents making the trip up to see him a few times a year.

It was better that way. He needed to be away from Texas. He was healthier and happier on his own—away from the smothering negativity and drama of his older brother, Phillip.

Evan didn't realize how much of a negative impact Phillip was having on his life until he left Galveston. He had grown by leaps and bounds in recent years. He had flourished since he moved to Nebraska. He grew as an athlete and a man. Evan missed the rest of his family, but Phillip had been a draining presence in his life since he was born, and Evan only realized the full impact of it when he moved away.

Evan was happy with his life in Nebraska. He had a lot of friends at college, and it was a game-changer to be able to pick and choose who he hung out with.

He was in his apartment, studying for a Biology test when he got the call.

Phillip had died.

His brother had passed away.

He was only twenty-three years old.

Evan could hardly remember the conversation. His mother had been the one to call. There was crying and vague explanations about an accidental drug overdose. Phillip had been through a lot of drug problems, so the news shouldn't have been that shocking to Evan.

But it was.

One minute, he was studying for a test, and the next, he was in his truck, headed down the horrifically open road from

Nebraska, through Kansas, Oklahoma, and then down through all of East Texas. It was a long trip. Evan left at 3pm and drove all afternoon, and then all night. He didn't get to Galveston until 7am the following morning, which meant he spent a total of sixteen sleep-deprived hours on the road.

It was impossible for him to sleep, anyway.

Phillip was gone. He was actually gone. Evan felt such conflicting emotions about it that his head was spinning.

Phillip had been through a lot of self-induced drama. It started with things like broken limbs from dare-devil stunts. He definitely had trouble with authority and it progressed to spells of drug use that had him in states where he could be considered a junky.

He'd been to the hospital at least 10 times for different things, but somehow the news of his passing still came as a complete shock to Evan. He was actually in shock from it. That had to be the term for what was going on with him. Or maybe it was just exhaustion from missing a night of sleep. Either way, Evan hardly remembered the sixteen-hour drive to Galveston.

His parents were up when he got to their house, and he drank a cup of coffee with them. His sister Lucy, the oldest sibling, was there, too, and she woke up not long after Evan arrived and joined them in the kitchen. Lucy was married with three kids. She and her husband, Drew, lived in Houston. Drew and their children had stayed back, but they would come in soon to attend the services.

Lucy and Phillip were adopted by Daniel and Abby King before Evan was born. Evan grew up thinking of them as his brother and sister and not even knowing that they were adopted.

His parents weren't the ones who told him. His cousin, Will, was the one who first let Evan know about his siblings. He did it when they were kids. Will was the same age as Evan and their mothers were sisters. Will had heard his parents talking about it and informed his cousin. Evan didn't care a thing about biological or not biological. It had nothing to do with blood type. Lucy was a good sister to him, and Phillip was not a good brother, that was all there was to it.

Phillip had an intense competitive streak, and since they were young children he had tried to beat Evan at everything. Evan was two years younger, and, for a while, Phillip was able to muscle him out. But from the age of about ten and up, Evan could compete with his brother and win at just about anything they tried.

Instead of this inspiring Phillip to get better and compete with Evan, it caused Phillip to look for other ways to beat Evan, such as lying about his own abilities or tearing Evan down. Phillip did these things in ways that other people wouldn't even notice. He made comments that only Evan could hear.

Evan was tenderhearted, and he had lived his life reacting to Phillip's narcissistic behavior. To put it bluntly, Evan constantly lessened himself to appease his brother. He wasn't able to date any of the girls he really wanted to date or enjoy accomplishments or victories because of how Phillip reacted to things like that.

Evan played football in high school, boxed at his uncle's gym, and had friends and girlfriends. From the outside, he lived a normal life. But his childhood and adolescence would have been totally different if Phillip had been a supportive older brother. Evan would have made completely different decisions.

Their mother, Abby, realized this and she made the extremely difficult decision to recommend that Evan go to college out of state. She videoed his football games and made a montage of him playing. She contacted the coaching staff at two dozen different schools with a heartfelt letter that said that Evan was not able to see his full potential in high school.

Evan had no idea his mother did that at the time. He just thought it was amazing that he got contacted by a division one school. He didn't get a scholarship or anything, but the coach at the University of Nebraska took a personal interest, saying that he would love to work with Evan. He gave him a guaranteed spot on the team, and that was good enough for the Kings.

Evan responded to his coach's style, and he began to make great strides as an athlete. He had been holding himself back for Phillip's sake all those years, and he was finally able to let go of that.

By his junior year, Evan worked his way up to a starting position and was earning a full scholarship. He was now a leader and driving force on a division one championship team.

Evan was able to live an unapologetic life in Nebraska. He didn't realize how smothering Phillip's presence had been until he was no longer around him. Evan loved his brother, but there had been countless moments in his life when he didn't like his brother at all. Years and years of misunderstanding and unhealthy competition had led to a strained relationship. He wrestled with guilt about this now that Phillip was gone.

Things had never been that way with Lucy. She and Evan were as close as any brother and sister could be.

Evan talked to his parents and Lucy while they all sat and ate breakfast. They spent the entire day together, just the four of them, talking, remembering, laughing, and crying. People stopped in—aunts, uncles, grandparents, cousins.

Evan talked a lot without saying much at all. He spoke with his family and added to the stories, but he left out so much of his own personal feelings that his head was spinning by the time the day was drawing to an end.

Spinning was the appropriate word for what Evan's head was doing. He was overwhelmed by his own thoughts and feelings. He spent a day seeing family, and he left the house at sunset to go sit on the beach and be by himself.

Lucy's husband, Drew, had a father who was a state senator. They owned a vacation home on the beach, and Evan told his family he was going there for some time alone. He knew he would need a place to crash, and people were constantly coming in and out of his parent's house, so he told them he might spend the night at the Senator's house.

No one questioned it. Lucy gave him the keys, and he took off. No one even realized how long it had been since Evan had slept. Everyone was so preoccupied with their own emotions that Evan's lack of sleep was somehow irrelevant.

It was the lack of sleep that sent him on a downward spiral that evening. It was as if he was in a drunken state, yet he had nothing to drink. Evan was sick from regret with the way he treated Phillip. He was sick about the fact that it had been weeks since he had called him. He had virtually cut Phillip off in recent years, and he was absolutely sick over it.

He went to the beach.

His family was too distracted to worry about stopping him.

Broken. Broken was the word for what Evan was. It wasn't like he was broken as in *broken down*—although he was that, too. But Evan was broken in the literal sense. He couldn't function properly. His mind didn't work right. Nor did his body. Nor did his emotions. It was a dark, cloudy, windy March evening, and Evan swam in the cold waters of the gulf. He didn't even feel the cold water. He had no idea how long he stayed in there. He swam for a mile or so before getting out of the water and walking back toward the Senator's house.

He didn't talk to anyone. It was chilly and dark, and he meandered down the shore toward the house. He stared downward, rarely looking up. Evan encountered strangers a few times who were out for walks, but they always kept their distance.

He stumbled from exhaustion. His body began to shut down as he made it back to the house. He was safe from the tide and far enough onto the private property that his body gave up and wouldn't carry him any further.

He collapsed the instant his brain registered that he was in a safe place.

Evan didn't even remember curling up in the beach grass that lined the path near Senator Klein's home.

He didn't remember falling asleep.

CHAPTER 2

Izabel Abbott (Izzy)
Later that same evening

I was back home in Galveston for a few days.

It was my mother's fiftieth birthday, and my sisters had planned a surprise party for her. The party would be at noon on Saturday, and I came home the day before so that I didn't have to make the four-hour trip from Corpus Christi so early that morning.

Seeing as how it was all a surprise, I opted to spend the night with my aunt and uncle. I drove in after work, so it was late when I got to their house. They greeted me and told me to make myself at home, but they went to bed not long after I got there.

Their home was in a beachfront community, and I wrapped a blanket around my shoulders and went for a walk along the shore to stretch my legs after spending hours driving. It was also nice to walk alone and listen to the waves and think—to clear my mind from the week at work.

My mom had texted me earlier to let me know that one of my classmates had passed away yesterday. I wasn't that close to Phillip King, but I went through school with him and knew his family. I worked at a news station where I was exposed to reports of all the bad stuff that happened in Corpus Christi and around the world, so I was somewhat desensitized to news of death, but it's just different when that happens to someone your age—someone you knew.

I walked for a long time, thinking about life, and mortality, and work, and tons of other things. I was at a stage in my career where I was pouring myself so wholeheartedly into my work and I brought it home with me. I always knew I wanted to be a television host, and I devoted myself to becoming the best at it. I began working at the news station during college. I started as an assistant to the producer, and now I had worked my way up to hosting the Meet Your Neighbor segment that aired live on weekdays, during the noon broadcast.

I had replaced the host, Ginger, once when she was sick. I filled in for a week, and the producer gave me the job. The station offered Ginger a different segment during the morning news, and she took it and was gracious enough considering it could have been really awkward.

It was my big break, and it had come by way of someone having strep throat. I had prepared for the moment when I got a shot, and I unapologetically tried my best to fill in for her. Meet Your Neighbor was the segment most suited for my personality, and I was pumped about taking over. I was, by a long shot, the youngest person on air at the station. I had been hosting the segment for six months, and I loved my job and took it seriously.

Even as I walked down the beach, I replayed things I said on the air earlier today, thinking about how I could improve and what I could change. I wasn't daydreaming about going out to clubs and trying to meet guys like most of my friends were. No, I was replaying the way I couldn't think of the word ambidextrous earlier today when I was talking to Jamie Neilson, head coach of a local high school baseball team.

No one knew I was having trouble coming up with the word. I blew past it and just talked about *using both your left and your right hand*, but it bugged me that a word left my mind while I was on camera.

It didn't matter in the long run. I knew I couldn't dwell on things that were in the past. But at the same time, I thought about it enough that I would probably never forget the word ambidextrous again.

It was late, and I knew I needed to get back to the house so that I could get some rest.

There was a man lying next to the path that led to Senator Klein's weekend home.

I couldn't see his upper body.

I had assumed he was there on purpose when I noticed him earlier. But it had been an hour since then, and it seemed as though he was in the exact same position. I knew it because I had already taken note of how flat-legged and sprawled-out he was.

I wondered if he was stargazing, and then I glanced up and saw that it was too cloudy for that. I figured he must be sleeping. I looked at the Senator's house. There was a truck parked in the driveway, but no lights were on in the house and it didn't look like anyone was home.

I bundled the blanket around myself as I tentatively walked a little closer to the man. I approached, staring at his foot, and watching to see if it might twitch. I had an over-active imagination, and I started to think of some scary things as I approached him. I had to walk right up to him and peer around some tall beach grass to get a good look at his face.

I peeked cautiously through squinted eyes, hoping and praying I'd see something normal.

It was.

It was just a guy sleeping.

No blood or anything.

Or so I thought he was only sleeping. I watched his body intensely to make sure I could see his chest rise and fall. It was slight, but I thought I could see it move.

I thought I could.

I squinted, watching him some more.

I went closer, stepping lightly on the packed sand of the path. I stared at his chest, and then my eyes roamed over his face. I peered closer when I thought I recognized him.

Was it...

Could it be...

I stepped closer to the man, moving to stand right over him now that I realized he looked familiar. It was dark out, but I knew the facial features.

Evan King. He was sleeping, and he had changed since I'd last seen him, but I definitely recognized his face. *Who was I kidding?* I knew his arms and legs, too. He was my forbidden crush for years. I had my eyes fixed on him all through school. I was two years older than him, so I never came out and told him I liked him, but I did like him, and I think he knew it.

But that hadn't worked out. He had a brother in my class, and I had been around him quite a bit. I hinted enough to give Evan a clue that I was interested, but he wouldn't give me the time of day. He blew me off more than once.

My heart actually ached a little when I realized this was Evan King lying there. He was the only guy I had ever liked who was younger than me. He was the only guy I'd ever flirted with and been blatantly rejected. He ended up dating a girl named Fran who was two years younger than him. I hadn't seen him in a few years.

It took a second for it to hit me that being Phillip's brother might have something to do with the fact that Evan was passed out. The house made sense, too. I had been away from Galveston for a long time, but I had family here, and I had heard enough gossip to know that Evan's older sister, Lucy, had married Senator Klein's son. I put the pieces together, and I reached down to touch his shoulder.

"Evan," I said, giving him a gentle shake. His shirt was damp. It was in the fifties outside. I couldn't believe he was sleeping out here in this weather. "Evan," I repeated.

Nothing. Nothing at all.

"Evan, wake up," I said, feeling a little worried about how unresponsive he was. I stooped down next to him and gave him another shake. "Hey, Evan."

Nothing.

I kneeled beside him cautiously. It was dark, but I could make out his facial features and I knew it was Evan.

"Hey, Evan," I said, trying to rouse him carefully.

Nothing.

I leaned in closer to him. He was breathing, but he seemed cold. I took the blanket off of my shoulders and covered him with it. I had no idea what I should do. I thought about trying harder to wake him up, shaking him. I thought it might be best to help him get into the house so he would be warm. I was relatively sure he wasn't sick or in danger. I thought he might've just ended up here because of what happened with Phillip. That thought made me wonder if he had been drinking. I leaned over him, and stretched downward, toward his face, trying to see if I smelled alcohol.

All I smelled was the beach.

"Evan," I whispered, staring down at him. "Evan, let me help you get to the house so you're not so cold out here."

I started to ask if he had the keys, but he was so unresponsive that I just quit talking. I stayed there for what must have been two full minutes, gazing at him and wondering what I should do. I hated to let him stay there, but I also hated to wake him up.

"Nooooo." Evan moved his head just slightly as he moaned the word. His voice was muffled and weak since he was talking in his sleep.

He grimaced, and I reached out to gently touch the side of his face.

"It's okay," I said, talking to him with his eyes closed. "Let's go in the house," I added now that he was stirring.

Evan moved. He reached out for me, latching on to me, curling into my side, and holding onto me like he expected me to protect him. He was a lot bigger than me, and he easily adjusted me, moving me next to him like I was his pillow. He held me tight and he began to shake a little. I thought it was from the cold, but then I realized that he was crying—little sobs in his sleep.

"Evan, it's okay," I whispered.

He latched onto me, holding me like I was a teddy bear. He shook and let out silent puffs of tears. It was an odd-sounding cry as if he was doing it in a dream.

"I wa-a-anted him dead. (muffled gasp) T-there were times when I wished it w-would ha-happen."

His words were barely intelligible, but I understood him through the mumbling haze. He sobbed again, that weird, shaking silent cry.

"But I didn't mean it," he moaned. "I was just mad. I'm sorry. I love you. I didn't want this to happen. I'm sorry I left you alone."

He spoke slowly and the words came out as a mumble while he slept.

"It's okay," I assured him. "You're okay."

I knew the King family well enough to know some of their dynamics. Phillip did not have an easygoing personality, and I knew Evan had done his best over the years to bridge the gap between Phillip and everyone else. Phillip gave Evan a hard time, but he loved him. I had run into him a couple of years ago, and he brought up Evan and the fact that he was away at college. He was proud of him and happy about him. Phillip had none of the kinds of hard feelings that seemed to be plaguing Evan right now. I knew it wasn't right for Evan to feel this kind of guilt.

"Phillip loved you," I promised, holding him, swaying with him. "He wasn't mad at all. You were a good brother, Evan, and he loved you."

He sobbed.

He latched onto me and cried in my arms. For a long time, Evan slept and moaned and cried and held onto me.

I talked back to him when he spoke, but I couldn't wake him. He never opened his eyes. I wanted to help Evan make it to his house so he didn't sleep outside, but there was just no pulling him from his slumber.

I didn't even consider leaving him.

I just didn't feel like it was an option with the state he was in.

I stayed awake for the longest time, curled up in the blanket and letting him hold onto me while he slept.

He didn't move once he got settled next to me. He shifted a little and talked and tensed up, but he never let go of me. He said things that were so sweet and heartbroken, that several times I tried to wake him up just to keep him from saying too much in front of me or being too hard on himself.

I just loved him.

I could easily be infatuated with a man like Evan, but this night was not about that. I held him and he held me, and it was strictly about comfort and peace and human contact. I kept him warm and held him when he cried. I comforted him emotionally and physically, and it had nothing to do with the fact that I could fall in love with him.

I stayed up for a long time, holding Evan King and telling him everything would be okay.

I fell asleep next to him.

I didn't mean to do it. I meant to leave during the night, but I stayed up with him so long that I opened my eyes to the sunrise. I flinched, but quickly realized where I was and that Evan King was still next to me, holding onto me.

I sat up, blinking.

"Evan," I whispered. "Hey, Evan," I said. I whispered again because I hated to wake him.

I could take my blanket and leave without a trace. I could say nothing, and no one would ever even know I had been there.

I looked up, over the grass, and realized I could see my aunt and uncle's house and other houses in the distance.

I considered telling someone Evan was out there. I thought of all my options, including calling the police or going to his parents to let them know where he was.

I stared at his face, which had a peaceful, neutral expression now. It looked like he was sleeping peacefully. It was a different expression than the one he had earlier when I first found him. I felt satisfied and content looking at him. I felt like he would be okay.

I decided I would go to my aunt's and take a shower and then I could come back and check on him in a little while. I considered taking the blanket so he wouldn't know I was there, but I left it on him. It was a blanket that my aunt had stored in the back of a closet, so I figured it wasn't important. I would buy her a new one if need be. Maybe I would come back out later and it would still be here. Either way, I wasn't taking it off of Evan. He looked comfortable and I left it on him.

I took a minute to do some thinking and consider my options, but I ended up getting up without even trying to rouse him again. I stood, staring down at him feeling much better about the way he looked now compared to the way he looked when I found him.

I felt like God had put me in the right place at the right time to help someone who really needed me. Thinking about God made me do something impulsive, something I normally wouldn't do.

I grabbed a nearby stick and stooped down, beginning to scratch words in the sand.

I wrote:

You are an amazing brother!

I knew Evan, and it was the truth. He was the youngest sibling, but Phillip had always looked up to him. He showed off that Evan was his brother. I knew I was writing the truth, and I knew it was something Evan needed to hear.

And then, without thinking, I added, *Phillip loved you and Jesus loves you, too!*

I drew fancy cursive letters combined with regular script. I drew a heart and a smiley face next to the words. The message fit perfectly on a little spot on the path and my handwriting came out even better than normal.

I almost bent down and erased it because it was not something I would normally do or say.

But I didn't have the heart.

It was its own little masterpiece, and I hated to get rid of it. Plus, Evan might not even see it if he stood up and walked the other way, toward the house. And if he did notice it, it was meant to be. I felt like he needed to hear those words after the night he had.

CHAPTER 3

Over a year later
Corpus Christi, Texas

It was a gorgeous evening in May and I was in a great mood. I recorded five extra segments this week so that I could take a vacation without anyone having to fill in for me.

I was settling into a routine at KRSM. I enjoyed my coworkers, and I felt like I was contributing to the team. I was thinking about one of my coworkers as I washed my hands.

Lance Reynolds.

He was the most well-known anchor at the station, and he was the reason I was out tonight. He had invited me for dinner and dancing with some of his friends. Lance was a popular anchor. He had a magnetic personality, and he knew a lot of people in Corpus Christi. He knew the chef in the restaurant at this busy downtown hotel, and that was how we ended up here for the night.

The hotel boasted an award-winning restaurant, and around the corner, there was a lounge area with a dancefloor and music. The place was packed with people enjoying the best of Corpus Christi's nightlife. There were about twenty of us in the group, a few from the station and some of Lance's other friends.

I wasn't there *with* Lance. We weren't seeing each other. His gaze had been holding mine a little longer lately, and he had invited me out with his friends tonight, but we weren't officially dating—neither of us had ever mentioned anything about that.

He was ten years older than me. I didn't see that as a problem, though. At least not as much of a problem as dating someone at work. He was the main anchor on the five and six o'clock evening news. I didn't have to work one-on-one with him at the station, but I ran into him all the time, at the beginning of his shift and the end of mine. I saw him enough that it would be really awkward if we dated and then broke up.

If I didn't work with Lance, I would definitely think about dating him, though. He was one of Corpus Christi's most eligible bachelors. I was honored to make it onto his guest list for the evening. He told me to dress up, so I wore an all-black sleeveless pantsuit with heels and a sheer black shawl with some silver and gold jewelry. It was dressy but not overdone. I was used to styled hair and wearing a lot of makeup to go on camera. I wore a little less tonight than I normally wore for work, but I still got dressed up for the evening.

I pulled my long, dirty blonde hair into a high ponytail, teasing and styling it to frame my face from behind me. I checked myself in the mirror at the hotel. There was white marble everywhere, and it looked lavish. The whole scene was perfect next to my outfit. I smiled into the mirror, feeling thankful for a fun night and good friends.

Seeing as how I wasn't the stay-out-all-night type, I knew I would probably do a little dancing, a few songs or so, and then head home. I had heard stories and was sure that some of this group would stay out late, but I had about another hour or two before my feet and shoulders began to hurt and I'd become tired and go home.

A group of young women came into the restroom as I walked out. They were all dressed up and smelled like perfume.

I smiled at them as I headed out.

I took a deep breath as I walked toward the restaurant. I knew I would go back to the section where our group was seated. We had a big u-shaped table with people sitting on the inside and out. People had been up and down, dancing and walking around, talking to others at our table and in the restaurant.

I had gone out of the restaurant and into the hotel lobby bathroom. It was a busy place, and I felt like I wanted a few seconds of quiet. I had to pump myself up on the way back to the restaurant. There were people in the hotel lobby, and I looked around, smiling at anyone who happened to be looking back at me. Only one person was, a lady, but she quickly looked away when our eyes met, so she missed my smile. I was walking as I looked at that lady, and after she looked away, I turned to continue down the hallway. Just then, I noticed two guys headed past me. They were both young men, tall and handsome. They were dressed like athletes in jeans and sneakers with t-shirts. One of them literally had the outline of a football on his shirt. It caught my eye. It was red and it said *Huskers* on it.

"Hey, the Cornhuskers!" I said as soon as it dawned on me that he was supporting Evan's team.

I knew that there was no cool way to say the word *cornhuskers*, but it came out of my mouth even nerdier than I imagined it would.

"I like Nebraska Football, too," I said, trying for some recovery as I walked past them.

I made eye contact with the guy wearing the shirt, and I was about to look at the other guy when I heard my name.

"Izzy Abbott."

Most of my friends called me Izzy, but random strangers who recognized me in public called me Izabel since that was what I went by on the air.

My eyes met his—the guy who said my name.

I felt flush as soon as I realized that it was Evan King.

Oh, goodness.

I had a major thing for him in school, and that whole episode on the beach a year before was still etched into my

24

mind like it had happened yesterday. I felt like I might actually collapse when I realized who it was.

"Evan King?" I said, looking as surprised as I felt. Shaking. I was shaking instantly.

We stepped back, getting out of the way of a group of people who were walking down the hall.

"Hey, Matt, I'll catch up with you in the room," Evan said, looking at his buddy who nodded and glanced at me before walking away.

Matt Walker, senior wide receiver for the National Champions Cornhuskers team. I knew exactly who he was. I nodded at the guy and we exchanged smiles as he walked off.

"What are you doing here, Izzy Abbott?" Evan asked, turning to me with a smile.

I could see him looking me over curiously, and I did my best not to blush, but it was impossible. He was more handsome than ever, and I felt speechless and breathless.

"I didn't know you were a Huskers fan," he added, smiling. "Is that what you said just now?"

"I am one," I said, nodding as confidently as I could. "I went to school with a guy on the team. I'm a big fan."

"Are you talking about me?" he asked, looking a little confused.

"No, there's this other guy who plays for the team who I also went to..." I grinned. "Yes, Evan, you. We went to school together, remember?"

"Of course I remember! Izzy Abbott. How are you? It's been a long time. You look amazing."

"Y-you too," I stuttered.

We were in the area leading from the lobby into the restaurant, and people constantly passed by us, so I stepped back a little.

"Do you really watch football?" he asked.

I nodded. "I missed most of the other seasons you played, but I watched all I could this past season. It was exciting. I couldn't get access to all of your earlier games, but once you made the playoffs, yeah, I think I watched them all. I was rooting for you, big time."

He stared at me like he was surprised and lost in thought.

"How are you with… I heard about Phillip. I'm sorry about that."

"Oh, it's okay," Evan said with a regretful smile. "He always had the biggest crush on you," he added.

"Who, Phillip?" I asked, laughing a little, nervously.

"Yes," Evan said. "Gigantic."

"I didn't even know," I said.

I didn't. I had been busy noticing Evan anytime I was around Phillip.

"What are you doing here?" he asked, looking around us.

"I live in Corpus Christi," I said. "For six years."

"I know that. I knew you lived here. Courtney told me."

"When did you see my sister?"

"A year or two ago. We talked for like fifteen minutes at the grocery store. She said you were working at a TV station. I remember you always wanting to do that. Are you still?"

"Yeah, yeah, I'm actually here with some people from the station. What are *you* doing here?"

"Oh, we're staying in this hotel—a few of us from the team. Matt's dad chartered us a boat that leaves tomorrow. We're going out fishing in the gulf tomorrow and then landing in Mexico for a few days."

"Oh, that's… wow… it's crazy running into you here. I never expected to run into you here. I, uh, I ran into Colleen Banks one time, but I usually never see Galveston people over here. It's weird. Well, I guess you're not in Galveston anymore."

"Yeah, I'm moving back there, actually," he said. "I finished up my finals. All I have to do is go back to Nebraska and graduate, and then I'm headed home."

"What are you going to do there? I thought you might try to play in the NFL. I heard a commentator say you could…"

"No," he said with a little laugh. "I had fun with football, but I'm going to quit while I'm ahead. Coach Hill wants me to help him out at the high school."

"So, you're going to work at the school? You're going to be a coach?"

"Well kind of. Just part-time, as a coach. I'll go on full-time with my dad at the hardware store."

"Is that what you want to do? "I asked.

"Yeah," he said. "I'm looking at it as a challenge. My cousin, Will, is working there, too, and we've got some ideas about how we can get into different markets and larger-scale distribution. I'm excited to work with him and my dad."

"Wow, I didn't know you were moving back." I paused, and for a second, we just stared into each other's eyes.

"You've always had the prettiest blue eyes," he said.

But I spoke at the exact same time, and my question was louder. "Did you guys eat at the restaurant?"

"No, we just came down to check it out—to see if we wanted to eat here or not."

"And? Do you?" I asked.

"Nah, it seemed a little fancy," he said. "We were kind of in the mood for a burger. Justin and Shawn want to go swimming later. I'm not sure what we'll decide about dinner. We might go out for a burger, or just get some room service."

"This restaurant has a really good burger," I said. "That's what I ate, and it was delicious. I already told myself I was coming back for another one sometime."

"You ate a hamburger in that outfit?" he asked, looking me over with a teasing expression.

I laughed. "Yes, I did. I picked it up with both hands and just bit right into it. A couple of people looked at me like I was crazy, but it was worth it. That burger was good."

Evan laughed.

I wanted to rewind to the part where he talked about my eyes, but it was too late to go back to that.

"What? You've never seen a girl eat a burger in four-inch heels?"

"Four inches?" he asked, disbelieving and looking down. "I thought you were looking taller than usual. I thought maybe you just grew since the last time I saw you."

"No, I'm still about like this," I said. I squatted down, putting myself what I thought was four inches shorter, but it might've been more like six. I smiled up at Evan, and he shook his head at me wearing an irresistible easy smile.

"Are you going to miss football?" I asked standing tall again.

Again, we talked over each other.

At the same time, he asked, "Are you in there... dancing?" He was looking me over with a serious expression as if appraising the situation.

"Yes," I said. "I danced once, and I might dance a few more times before I go home. I'm not staying out all night or anything. I'm tired from work."

"What are you doing, exactly, at the news station?"

"I have a little talk show segment during the news at noon. I feature local people with interesting stories or jobs. It's called Meet Your Neighbor."

"Oh, that's cool. You'd be perfect for that." He nodded thoughtfully. He was sweet and down to earth, and I was so happy to see him that I thought I might cry.

CHAPTER 4

*L*ance chose that moment to come out of the restaurant looking for me.

"There you are!" he called from a distance, causing both Evan and me to look his way.

And just like that, the Evan trance was broken, and I was snapped back to reality. I looked at Lance as he approached. He was one of the most handsome, popular people in Corpus Christi, and he was headed my way, looking for me. I should have been excited. But I was disappointed. I did not want my conversation with Evan to end. I couldn't believe I had run into him, and I was too shaken up by the encounter to relax and enjoy talking to him.

I couldn't help but compare the two of them as Lance drew near. The gentlemen were both good-looking, but there was no comparing the two. Evan was simply the perfect man. Lance was dressed sharply in a suit and people would argue that no one could possibly be better looking, but that wasn't the case—and it was obvious next to Evan. They were both handsome with slender, athletic builds, but Evan held himself differently than Lance. There was something about Evan's natural swagger and confidence.

I would never see Lance the same again now that he had stood next to Evan. I was learning, in this moment, that Evan King ruined every man he stood next to. *Note to self: if I ever got married, I could never introduce my husband to this man.*

Lance looked at Evan and stuck out his hand as he came closer. "Lance Reynolds," he said in that proud way that made me know he assumed Evan would recognize him.

"Evan King," Evan returned, shaking Lance's hand.

"I know Evan from Galveston," I said. "We went to school together."

"Oh, you like Nebraska, too?" Lance said, gesturing to Evan.

Evan had on a grey t-shirt, and I didn't even see that it had the word Cornhuskers printed in tiny letters on the sleeve until Lance motioned to it and asked about Nebraska.

"This girl is *crazy* about that team," Lance added.

He put his hand on my back. He tried to make it a way to gesture to me as he was talking about me, but I flinched a little at his touch.

I tried to discreetly step away as I looked at him and replied to his comment. "What makes you say that?" I asked.

"Because *all winter*, every time you're off the air, you're wearing that big, honking red sweatshirt."

I could feel myself starting to blush, and I began thinking about cotton candy, which was what I always did when I felt myself blushing and needed to regain my composure.

I imagined spinning the sweet sticky fibers onto a paper cone. I had worked the cotton candy machine one summer on the boardwalk in Galveston, and I always found escape in the memory of watching the pastel fibers spin and stick to each other.

"I got into football this year," I said, smiling calmly and with a shrug. "Evan plays for Nebraska, and if I'm going to be watching football, I'd like to cheer for a team where I know someone playing."

"Oh, you play for that team?" Lance asked.

Evan nodded. "Yes, sir."

"That's great," Lance said, nodding. "You all did pretty well this year, didn't you?"

"We did, we won the title," Evan said.

"Well, that explains why Izzy never took that sweatshirt off," Lance said, laughing. "Hey, it was nice meeting you, but if you'll excuse us..." Lance looked at me. "I was just talking to Sheila. She said if you want to get that interview with Travis Wilson, you should try to go talk to him in person. He's here with his wife and the woman who runs the ACC. Millie caught sight of them a minute ago. She said they were almost done eating, and I don't know if they'll stay much longer after that."

"Oh, okay," I said, nodding. "Thank you."

"I'll let you go," Evan said. "I don't want to keep you from your meeting. But was great seeing you, Izzy. I'm happy to see you're doing so well." He looked at Lance with a little nod. "Nice meeting you," he added.

"Likewise, Evan."

"I'm sorry we didn't get to talk more," I said, looking at Evan with as much regret and sincerity as I could pack into a three-second smile. I felt disappointed, but then I remembered he was moving back to Galveston. "But I guess you'll be at the hardware store," I added. "I can swing by and say 'hi' when I'm in town."

"I'd love that," Evan said.

I took a deep breath, and smiled again as I reached out to hug Evan. He came toward me and hugged me back. He was even bigger than he was last year on the beach. I remembered him holding onto me that night. I ached at the memory.

Evan hesitated with me in his arms, hugging me for a heartbeat longer than I expected him to. He looked at me with a somewhat intense expression when we pulled away. His expression seemed slightly confused, and I tilted my head at him.

"It was s-so nice seeing you," he said, stuttering and looking a little dazed.

"It was great seeing you, Evan. Really. I mean it."

Lance put his hand on my back again, and I lunged away, reaching out to hug Evan again like that had been my plan all along.

"It's been way too long!" I said, explaining the second hug. "Don't be a stranger."

"You either," Evan said, giving me a squeeze. He looked at me and then at Lance. I could tell he thought we were together. I wanted to explain, but it was just too awkward with Lance standing right there, waiting. *Why in the world would Lance have chosen this night to make a possessive gesture like that? What was he doing?*

I was mad at first, and I thought about it as we walked away from Evan. I asked myself how I would've felt if Lance had touched my back on a night when I wasn't standing in front of Evan.

I couldn't say.

All I knew was that it was horrible timing.

I went through the motions after that.

I followed Lance to the table, and then I went to talk to Travis Wilson. Lance came with me. He was higher profile than I was, and Travis didn't hesitate to welcome Lance to their table. Lance introduced me as the host of the Meet Your Neighbor segment, and I told Travis I'd love to have him on the show.

I didn't get a definite answer, but the interaction went really well, better than I ever expected. He gave me a woman's name and told me to get in touch with her for scheduling. I was excited and in a good mood as I went back to the table with Lance. I smiled and thanked him and said all the right things but I could not stop thinking about Evan.

I thought maybe before I left for the evening I could stop by the front desk and ask for his room number. That way I could maybe call and… but no. That would never work. I couldn't just randomly look up Evan and call him just because he was staying the night in my town. *Or could I? Was it a big deal that I had run into him? It felt like a big deal.*

I wanted to talk to him, but I didn't think it was going to happen. I made the conscious choice to go on with my evening.

The restaurant wasn't quiet, but it got even louder as Lance and I walked around the corner to get to the section where there was dancing. Club music was pumping through the speakers, and there were lots of people, dressed to the nines, dancing and swaying. Lance had a reputation for being a partier, and he was instantly surrounded by a group of eight or ten people when he went out there. He didn't touch me, but he danced next to me, and he made eye contact quite a bit.

And then I saw Evan from across the room.

He was standing next to some tables, looking around, searching.

I stopped dancing the instant I saw him. I peered through the crowd. It was packed in there, and I stared intently to make sure it was Evan. It definitely was. There was no mistaking him. I didn't know if he was looking for me, but there was nothing I could do to stop myself from going toward him.

I motioned to Lance with one finger in the air, letting him know I'd be right back. He smiled and nodded, turning to dance with his friends.

When you're at home, watching the news, you'd never dream that the composed man who sat in a suit and read the news reports would also go out on Saturday night and rip it up and get all sweaty on the dance floor. But there he was. Lance Reynolds—professional news anchor and club-scene aficionado.

I left him there, and walked toward Evan. He was looking the other way, checking out tables. He didn't see me coming from the direction of the dance floor. It was dark in there, and different color lights were flashing in time to the music. I went straight for Evan, wondering what he was doing.

I was only about ten feet away when Evan turned and saw me. He smiled, looking relieved.

"Hey!" I yelled over the music. I came near him wearing a smile that I hoped was casual and didn't reflect how very excited I was to see him.

"Hey," Evan said, leaning in to speak closer to my ear. "I know you're busy, and you're here with your—"

"He's not my… I'm just here with some people from work," I said. "And I'm not busy."

"Would you walk into the restaurant with me for a second so we don't have to yell?"

"Sure," I said without even thinking about it.

And the two of us walked out of the loud room and into the quieter one. There was a big partition in the middle of the dining room with large fish aquariums built into it, and Evan went to stand next to the end of one of them so that we could be out of the way.

"I'm sorry to interrupt you," he said.

"Please don't be," I insisted. "I'm happy you came. I'm happy to see you."

"I had to ask—I wanted to ask you something." He stared at me, blinking.

"Yeah, sure. Anything."

"C-can I, would you, uh, mind if... do you think I could h-hug you again, Izzy? I was hoping to smell something."

I held eye contact with him as I cautiously leaned down and sniffed my own shoulder area. "I hope I don't stink," I said.

"Nooo," he said, looking serious. "It's just, earlier when you and me... you hugged me earlier, and I have this blanket. This blanket that... G-God gave me. I know that's weird of me to say, but there's a blanket that I thought smelled like God, and it turns out it smelled like you. You smelled like God. I mean, I don't know if you... I'm not trying to say you... but it's the same smell." He paused and stared at me like he was sorry for rambling and being so confusing but he didn't know quite how to say what he wanted to say. "I know all of this sounds completely crazy. It sounds crazy coming out of my mouth,

and I'm the one standing here saying it. But do you mind if I...
just... smell... you... for a second, Izzy?"

"No," I said. "Not at all."

Evan stepped closer to me, leaning in. He put his face next to
my neck, he wasn't touching me, but we were definitely sharing
space. I could feel his body heat. I was breathless. I literally held
my breath while he was that close to me. He drew air through
his nose, taking a long breath in. His nose touched my neck,
and I wanted it to stay there so badly that I didn't flinch at all.
Evan stayed still for several more seconds, breathing in again,
and then he pulled back and looked me straight in the eyes.

"What is that smell?" he asked intensely.

"I don't know. My perfume, maybe?"

"What kind of perfume is it?"

"Angel."

"I knew it. I told you."

"No, it's *called* Angel. That's the name of the perfume."

"That's the name of it?"

"Yeah. It's in a star bottle." I brought my shirt up to my nose
and smelled it. "I didn't even think you could still smell it on me."

"It's just regular perfume?" Evan asked, stunned.

"Yes," I said. "I got it at the mall."

CHAPTER 5

Evan

*H*is head was spinning after that encounter with Izzy Abbott in the hotel lobby. He was now and had always been devastatingly attracted to this girl. And here she was, looking exquisite—less like a girl and more like a woman.

And to top it all off, she smelled like God.

Evan had an encounter with God on the beach after his brother's death. He slept on the sand, and God had been there and had comforted him. As if the experience of actual physical comfort wasn't enough, there was a blanket over him and a message etched in the sand.

Evan had kept that blanket. He had shaken out the sand but he wouldn't dare wash it because of the smell. He knew there was a chance that some human had placed the blanket on him and written the message, but his brain associated that smell with God, therefore Izzy Abbott smelled like she had God's scent on her.

Evan felt like he wanted to take a hold of Izzy and never let her go. But he suspected he would want that no matter what she smelled like. She was the woman of his dreams, his main crush for most of his life.

He was insanely jealous of her boyfriend. It was the weirdest sensation. Phillip had always had a thing for Izzy, and because she was Phillip's classmate, Evan had given in and kept himself from looking at her or responding to her when she tried to talk to him. He was jealous of Phillip for that even though the two of them never dated. Evan wanted Izabel then and he wanted her now.

He couldn't believe this smell. He couldn't believe he had run into Izzy all these miles from home. He couldn't believe she wore a Nebraska sweatshirt. *Was there a chance that she had been thinking about him all these years?* He felt like he wanted to be next to her. He wanted to stare at her and get to know more about her.

"I know you're out with your friends—" he started to say.

But she cut him off when she heard that, speaking quickly and nervously. "No, no, no, I don't care about them. I mean, I, y-yes, I care about... but I'm not, I'm here by my, I drove here by myself."

Evan stared at her, trying to take it all in, trying to think of the right thing to say. "I thought you were with your boyfriend," he said, since he had to know.

"Lance isn't my boyfriend."

Evan stared at her. There was music and murmuring and clanking of dishes and all sorts of noise swirling around them, but to him, it seemed silent. Izzy was wearing all black and it was dark in the room, but her honey blonde hair and blue eyes shone and sparkled. She denied that the other man was her boyfriend and she did it in such a way that Evan felt hope, like she might want to see him again.

He stared straight into her eyes as he spoke. "I was on my way out to eat with my friends, but we'll be back in just a little while. Do you think you'll still be here?"

"Yeah, yeah, definitely," she said, smiling. "Why? Would you want to try to h-hang out or something?"

Evan pulled back and grinned and stared at her. "That's what I came here to ask you," he said.

"You did?"

He nodded.

His heart was pounding.

"Yeah, I'd love to," she said.

This sent a wave of warmth and electricity through Evan's body. He wanted to take her then and there. He had been so focused on school and football that he had made the conscious decision not to date women. But now he was ready to get married. *Was he really thinking about getting married? Was that what this girl did to him?* He couldn't believe she wasn't spoken for. He ached to claim her.

He cleared his throat. "I'm, uh, we'll be back in an hour or so. Where should I meet you?" Evan wanted to ask her if she would go with him now, but the guys had rented a truck and barely had room for everyone who was going. Plus, they were already in the truck waiting and had given him a hard time about going back inside in the first place.

"Maybe in the lobby?" she asked.

Evan looked at his watch. "Let's say ten o'clock in the lobby. Will that work?"

It would be over an hour, but Evan wanted to make sure she didn't have to wait.

"Ten's fine. Ten's great," Izzy said.

"I think Shawn was talking about swimming if you want to do that. The pool's open late."

"Oh, really? Is that what you're doing, too?"

"I, we could. Would you want to?"

"Oh, me? I don't have a swimsuit here," she said.

Evan started to tell her that it was okay and that they could just have coffee or go for a walk, or do something else, but she spoke again.

"I can probably get one while you're eating," she said. "If we're not meeting till ten, I could just run home."

"I don't want to make you leave your friends," he said.

"I really don't mind," she assured him. "I would look forward to catching up with you, Evan."

The sound of his name coming off of her lips made his chest feel tight.

"Good," he said, knowing he needed to be in a hurry since his friends were waiting. He reached out for a hug, and Izzy came willingly into his arms. For goodness sake. He could just squeeze her until she disappeared.

"I've got to go," he said breaking the hug and starting to leave. "But please be back here at ten."

"I will!" she said, smiling at him.

Evan could hardly concentrate on what he was doing when he walked away from Izzy. He felt like he might need a cold shower to get his mind right.

He went to get some food with his friends, and she was so in the forefront of his mind that he talked about her to them while they were eating. There were four others from the team, five guys, including Evan. They all sat around a table, eating together like they had done lots of times before.

There was a certain comradery that came with playing on the same sports team. And by the time you make it to the championship level, like these gentlemen, you give so much of yourself to the sport that your teammates are like family.

They went out to eat burgers, and Matt ordered a thirty-piece platter of chicken wings as an appetizer. All of them dug in except for Evan, who was preoccupied.

"Izzy Abbott," he said. "She was in my brother's grade. Phillip used to talk about how much he liked her—like he had dibs on her or something. Everybody liked her, though, I don't know why I thought Phillip really had a…" Evan trailed off when he realized he didn't even need to finish the sentence. "She was the homecoming queen and prom queen and all that. And she was smart. I think she got student of the year for the whole state one time."

"Wasn't your brother older than you?" Matt asked.

"Yeah. Two years. Which is another reason she seemed out of reach back then."

"E-King, going for the older ladies," Jesse said using Evan's nickname in a teasing tone.

"Two years is nothing," Evan said.

"Yeah, that's nothing," Matt agreed.

"She's on TV, I think. She's hosting some kind of talk show segment on the news."

"A talk show?" Matt asked.

"I think. Something about meeting your neighbor. We only got to talk for about twenty seconds. I thought she had a boyfriend because she was there with this Tom Cruise looking guy."

"But he wasn't her boyfriend?" Matt asked.

"I don't think so, no. I thought he was, though. He shook my hand, and I almost shot in and tackled him."

The guys laughed at that.

"Since when is *Mister Single* trying to bag a lady?" Shawn said, chewing on a chicken wing.

"I'm not trying to *bag* anyone," Evan said. "Whatever that means. This girl is different. She's the girl next door. The one you take home to meet your mama."

"Not tonight, though," Matt said.

"Tonight, she's taking a dip with my boy Evan in the pool," Shawn added.

They all laughed. Evan had already told them that she might come swimming with them. "Seriously, though," Evan said. "Don't mess with her too much. She's a good girl. I don't want her to think I'm…"

"Whew, son! That boy's already whipped!" Shawn said, smiling and shaking his head and making them all laugh.

"It's about time Evan gets himself a lady," Matt said.

"What does she look like?" Shawn asked.

"Like your mom," Justin said, messing with Shawn who rolled his eyes.

"I saw her," Matt said. "She looks good."

"She's blonde. Dirty blonde," Evan said.

"Real blonde or fake blonde?" Shawn asked.

"It doesn't matter," Jesse said. "All blonde is good blonde."

"I don't know if it's real or fake," Evan said. "I wouldn't even know how to tell that."

"You can tell if the whole hair is one color," Jesse said.

"What?" Evan asked, glancing at him with a confused expression.

Jesse motioned to his own head. "Her hair. If it's real blonde, it's all the same color, if it's fake blonde, there's all kinds of different colors mixed in there."

"I don't think that's how it works," Matt said.

"I have no idea about her hair," Evan said. "Other than it's perfect."

The guys made various noises of approval at Evan's comment.

"Didn't you say you went to elementary school with her?" Matt asked. "What color was her hair back then?"

"Light," Evan said. "Like it is now. Pretty much. I can't tell. I don't look at that stuff other than to know it looks good. It was pulled back in a ponytail, and it was blonde. That's all I know."

"She's gotta look good if she has Evan King all messed up and talking about ponytails," Shawn said, making them laugh.

"She does look good," Evan said.

He wanted to say it wasn't about that. He started to tell them it was so much more than that. But that was the kind of statement that'll get a man laughed at in front of a bunch of football players. So, Evan kept it to himself.

"You'll see what she looks like," he said. "You'll get to meet her in a minute."

CHAPTER 6

Izzy

Evan had come to look for me.

He thought I smelled like God, and I was too stupefied to tell him any different. It crossed my mind to tell him that there was a perfectly good explanation as to how the blanket got on him that night and why it smelled the way it did. But I couldn't say anything. It never felt like it was the right moment to let that come out of my mouth, so I had kept it inside.

The truth was, I was thankful for the whole perfume thing. It was the factor that made him come look for me. It was the reason I had left my friends and gone home to change into a swimsuit. I bid Lance and the rest of them a good evening and went straight home to change after I talked to Evan.

It took fifteen minutes to get my car out of the valet, and another twenty minutes for me to drive home, so I felt a little frazzled the whole time I was changing. But I figured maybe that was just the excitement of it all.

I put on a one-piece swimsuit under some jeans and a short sleeve blouse. It was a Bodyglove brand bathing suit, all black with a little stripe detail along the seams. I traded in my heels for a pair of flats and I left my hair in a ponytail. I made it back to the hotel fifteen minutes early, and I found an out-of-the-way place to sit in the lobby while I waited for Evan.

He and his friends were five minutes late. That obviously wasn't a big deal, but seeing as how I was fifteen minutes early, it seemed like a long time. And given how badly I wanted to see Evan, twenty minutes might as well have been an eternity.

I watched the direction that came from the elevator, and I watched the door that led outside. Lots of people came in and out, but none of them were Evan.

And then he appeared. There were five of them, all tall, strapping men, athletes. Evan caught sight of me from across the room when I stood. He gave me a smile and began to head my way. He walked faster than the others, and I watched him the whole time, only vaguely aware that the other guys were trailing behind him. I was so excited to see Evan. It was crazy that he was in Corpus Christi and even crazier that I had run into him.

I was so happy to see him that I felt like I could cry. I stood up straight and tall, giving him my best confident greeting. "Hi there," I said as he got closer.

"Hey, I'm sorry. We would have been here sooner, but everyone decided to stop at a gas station on the way back."

"Don't be sorry," I said. "I haven't been here long."

"You changed clothes," he said, looking me over.

I was about to answer and agree with him, but his friends came up to us, and one of them spoke before I could.

"I have to meet the lady who had Evan rushing me at the restaurant."

The guys came up behind Evan. The tallest, biggest one was the one who said it. Shawn Culpepper, the number one linebacker in the country.

"Bull, I did not rush you," Evan said. "You had sixty-two chicken wings and two double cheeseburgers. How much more food can one man eat?"

They were ribbing each other, and Shawn leaned in and punched Evan's shoulder. "This is Shawn, Justin, and Jesse," Evan said, pointing toward Shawn and the others but looking at me. "And you met Matt earlier, right?"

"Briefly," I said. I waved at Matt. "I'm Izzy." I gave them all a wave as I looked from one guy to the next. I felt like I was part of the huddle with them all standing near me like this. "It's nice to meet all of you," I continued. "I'm Izabel Abbott. Evan and I grew up together, in Galveston."

"Evan was telling us all about that," Jesse said.

"He said you were the prom queen," Shawn said.

I was a princess at the prom, not the queen, but I wasn't going to correct him. I was the homecoming queen, so that was probably what Evan remembered.

"Oh, that's been a few years," I said, smiling and making light of his comment.

The guys said something to each other while Shawn and I had that exchange, and within a minute, they decided to go to the restaurant for dessert. Really, it was just because it was busy in there and they wanted to check out the ladies, but they blamed the idea on eating dessert.

Evan offered to skip it if I didn't want to go along, but I told him I didn't mind. I didn't want him to miss out on anything with his friends.

Jesse wrangled a group of ladies at a nearby table who wanted to hang out. They were nice enough—some young teachers from a local elementary school who were there celebrating a birthday. We squeezed around the booth and brought two extra chairs so everyone could fit. The ladies were nice, and it was not a surprise to any of us when Jesse invited them to come swimming.

They readily agreed. I could tell they were excited to talk to the guys. There were five of them and five guys, but Evan was out of the equation. He was completely focused on me. There was no question in anyone's mind about that. He was always looking at me and talking to me and making sure I was comfortable.

One of the girls lived on this block, and three of them left to go to her apartment and get swimsuits for everyone. We stayed in the restaurant to wait for them, but we all agreed that we would go swimming as soon as they got back.

We sat there for a few minutes before Jesse and Justin decided to go use the restroom. Evan and I stood up to let them get out of the booth.

I was in the middle of all that when Lance from work came up to our table.

He had taken off his jacket, unbuttoned his shirt at the neck, and rolled up his sleeves. I could tell that he had been dancing because he was sweaty.

"Oh, my goodness, Lance Reynolds, *K-R-S-M!*" The girl, Michelle was her name, sang the jingle. The two remaining women at our table were locals, and they obviously recognized Lance, because they were beaming. One of them said something about recognizing me earlier, too, but they were starstruck by Lance.

"Nice to meet you," Lance said with a fleeting smile before turning to me. Evan and I were both still standing up from having let Jesse out of the booth, and Lance stepped to the side to talk to me. "What are you doing here?" he said. "Millie saw you from over there, and I was like, that can't be Izzy. But here you are." He reached out to hug me. "Was this the same night you were here with me? Weren't you wearing something different earlier?"

"Yeah, I went home to change, and then we met back up—Evan and me. I didn't even know if you'd still be here."

"Oh, yeah, we're just getting started," Lance said. "Why don't you come back in there with me?"

I could feel myself blushing as I tried to maneuver the situation. "Oh, no, thank you. I'm going to stay here with these guys. We were about to… head out." I turned a little and gestured to Evan. "This is Evan. You met him earlier."

It was a little awkward of me to introduce them again, but I wanted to acknowledge Evan and I didn't know how else to do it.

"We met," Evan said, with a nod. He gave Lance a smile, but it was forced.

"Yeah, we sure did," Lance said. "The Cornhuskers. Are all of you football players?" Lance asked the question as he turned to look at everyone who was still at the table, and the guys all nodded, agreeing that they were.

We had a few more exchanges about football and Lance being a newscaster at my station before Lance walked away. I slid into my place at the booth, and Evan sat next to me.

Everyone was talking. The girls were excited about seeing Lance, which made the guys feel competitive and set them off on a session of talking smack and showing off.

Evan wasn't a part of it. He was quiet as he got settled in next to me. "I'm ready to get out of here," he said, looking at me.

"Are you okay?" I asked.

"Yeah," he said smiling.

But he wasn't quite telling the truth. Something was on his mind.

"Are you sure?" I asked.

Evan nodded. He sat up in his seat, joining in on the conversation since everyone was talking about the boat trip they were going on the following day.

"We're leaving out on the boat tomorrow, and heading all the way to Port Isabel," Matt said. He looked at me. "Do you know where that is?"

"Down on the Mexican border," I said.

Matt nodded. "My dad works in this area, so he has connections down here. We'll take the boat to Port Isabel and then drive down to Mexico from there. My dad's boss has a house on the beach, and we'll stay for a couple of days. I've been there once before. It's crazy. They have servants."

"That sounds amazing," Michelle said.

I looked at Evan who gave me a little smile. "And then we go back to school for one week before graduation," Evan said to everyone.

"So, none of you are from Texas?" Michelle asked.

"I am," Evan said. "Galveston."

The girls had both been to Galveston and they responded with stories of their experiences there.

We were still talking about it when the others came back to the table. We paid our tab and all got up to head upstairs.

I didn't mind hanging out with those girls while we changed. They were friendly and funny, and it was no big deal for me to be apart from Evan for ten minutes. There was a small women's locker room and restroom, and I left my outfit in there on my way to the pool area. It was gorgeous—lush and tropical, lined with palms and banana trees and flowers.

I saw Evan the second I walked into the pool area. He and two other guys, Shawn and Matt, were together. Evan was sitting on the side of the pool with his feet dangling in the water, and the other two were already swimming. Michelle and two other girls both shrieked with excitement and jogged past me, headed straight for the pool. It was huge, and L-shaped, and they took off in the direction of Jesse and Justin, who were swimming on the other side. I had picked up a towel in the locker room, and I went to put it on a chair near Evan where I could see his shoes.

I was nervous. Evan had always been one of the guys who didn't mind taking his shirt off in the summer. I had seen him bare-chested before. But he had filled out since he had been off at college, and I could hardly look at him without feeling all hot and bothered. I blushed and I thought of cotton candy as I stashed my towel on the chair.

I assumed Evan was watching me, and I turned around to see that my assumptions were true. He was in the pool now, closer to me, and he was alone, staring up at me with a smile.

His head was wet, and I imagined him slipping into the pool and swimming a whole lap underwater behind my back.

"How'd you get over here so fast?" I asked.

Evan smiled up at me. "I just swam. Come on in," he said. "The water's amazing."

CHAPTER 7

*E*van swam away from the side of the pool, making a little space for me to get in. I put my toes to the edge and then I sat down gently, letting my legs dangle in the water.

"What are you waiting for?" Evan asked, treading water and smiling up at me. The pool had underwater lights, and I could see his body through the water. It was blurry, but I could still make out his shape and the lines of his muscles.

Goodness gracious.

Oh my.

He might as well have been a real king, and not just by last name. He was perfect, and he was staring up at me with a smile. I had no idea what his story was. He could have ten girlfriends in Nebraska for all I knew. He could just want to hang out with me for a night while he was in Corpus Christi. I had no idea what he was thinking.

"Izzy, come on in," Evan said.

"I'm scared," I admitted.

"Of what? I know you can swim."

"Yeah, but I've never been in a pool on a rooftop."

"Yeah, so? What difference does that make?"

"Do you think it can... hold all this weight?" I asked, looking around.

Evan laughed and pushed away from the side. He had grown up in the water and he laid on his back, swimming and looking like a playful otter, waiting for me.

"I thought you were going to say you were scared of lightning or something—something coming out of the sky—not of the weight. I promise the pool won't collapse when you get in it. Is that what you think?"

I nodded, being tender and serious.

"Really?" he said sweetly. He reached up, offering a hand to help me into the pool. "It's no more weight with you being in here than it is with you being on the side right there. You might as well get in."

I took his hand and popped off of the side and into the water gently. I smiled when I figured out that my feet could touch, just barely. I latched on the edge of the pool and glanced at the side. The closest indicator said the water was five feet deep, which made sense.

"I'm in," I said nervously, holding onto Evan's hand with one hand and the edge of the pool with the other. I let go of Evan's hand when I realized that it was me who was squeezing him. "Thank you," I said. "For helping me in." I shivered and turned to him, letting my legs flow in the water.

He came closer to me. "I never dreamed you'd be scared," he said.

My arm touched his as we swam underwater.

"I'm not scared of swimming at all," I said. "I've just never been in a pool on a roof before. I didn't even know these existed. How is this possible? Doesn't this water weigh like a million pounds?"

"Probably," he said. "Not a million, but a lot. But they know what they're doing. I would have never even questioned it."

"Have you been in one of these before?"

Evan nodded and absentmindedly wiped his wet face. "A few times," he said. "We stay in nice hotels when we travel. Especially for bowl games."

"Well, I've never been in one. I thought you were joking when you said for us to meet you up here."

"I thought you went to places like this all the time. You know, with your fancy TV job."

"No," I said with a laugh. "The studio is about the only place I go with my job. This was my first time even going out with those people. I've never even been to this hotel before."

"Were you here with that guy tonight?"

"Who, Lance?"

"Yes, Lance."

"No."

"He touched you like you were."

"I don't know why he did that."

"Did what?" he asked making sure we were on the same page.

"Why he held my back like that," I said.

Evan didn't say a thing.

Right after I mentioned Lance touching my back, Evan sucked in air and then he ducked and went under the water. I watched as he pushed off, darting quickly through the water, away from me. He swam like a fish underwater, all the way to the other side of the pool. He came up, and then slowly shook the water from his hair and turned to look at me.

"Where'd you go?" I asked, calling to him from across the pool. There was music and talking, and I had to yell for him to hear me.

"Over here," he said.

"Come back!" I yelled.

"You come here," he said.

I was prepared for this. I had already taken off any makeup that would run and smear. I still wasn't sure about the pool on a rooftop, but I chose to forget about it. I pretended that it was nice and underground, like any proper pool should be. I went underwater, and just the same as Evan did, I shot about halfway across the pool swimming to the other side.

I was nervous and I didn't get a good breath, so I had to come up several feet from the side. That was fine, because otherwise, I would've run into Evan. I was able to touch, just barely, and I swam forward with my head out of the water to latch onto the side of the pool.

"Why did you swim away?" I asked, settling in a spot next to him.

"Because I had to cool off," he said. "I don't want to think about a guy's hand on your back."

Right after he said that, Evan instantly went under and swam to the other side. He came up. "Stay there. I'll come back to you," he said from the other side.

Within a few seconds, Evan swam to me again.

He came up for air next to me, which was right next to the wall.

"I'm sorry," he said, soaking wet and catching his breath. "I have to cool off when I think about it."

I knew all of this "cooling off" stemmed from Evan being Jealous over me, and it was honestly a glorious feeling. I propped my upper back against the edge, looking into the pool. Evan settled next to me, facing the other way, holding onto the side and facing away from the pool.

We made eye contact. I had let my hair down in the locker room, and it was floating all around my shoulders in the water. We had talked a lot at the table, catching each other up on our lives, but we had said nothing about dating or relationships.

"Is it safe to assume there's no Mrs. Evan King?" I asked.

"What's that mean?" he asked, looking at me. He had droplets of water on his face and neck and shoulders, and I could hardly look at him without wanting to lean in—cling to him.

"You know," I said. "Isn't there a lady who's waiting for you in Nebraska?"

He smiled wryly at me. "You think I'm married and I'm over here, checking you out in your swimsuit?"

"Oh, I didn't know you were checking me out," I said.

"You didn't?" he asked. "Then I'm not doing a good job."

Evan swiveled, coming to stand directly in front of me, trapping me against the side of the pool. I took an uneven breath, leaning against the edge and peering at him. The lights and waves caused shadows to play across his face and body.

"I am definitely checking you out, Izzy. I've been doing that for most of my dang life."

I laughed at the way he said it, but then it hit me what he was saying. "No, you haven't," I said, squinting at him. "I tried to blatantly hold your hand at Billy Freeman's party and then again at the cemetery that night after we all went trick-or-treating with Jenny and Josh."

"That night at the cemetery, you just bumped into me," he said.

I laughed, since that was pretty accurate. "In my mind, I sat there and tried to hold your hand for an hour," I said.

"I remember Billy Freeman's party," he said. "It was the pool party. Phillip was right there next to me the whole time. He liked you, and you two were the same age, so I just…"

"You don't have to say it," I said. "I understand. I'll just tell myself you *would have* held my hand at Billy's pool party that day under different circumstances."

Evan came closer to me. Our bodies weren't touching, but there was not a lot of space between us. We were so close that we had to work at *not* touching each other. The water shifted around us, and I yearned to hold onto him.

"I would have easily held your hand that day," he said, slowly, seriously. "I would have held it that day and lots of other days."

He reached out and touched me lightly. Both of his hands, coming around my waist. I was glad for the distraction of the water because my heart was pounding. It was a surreal moment. A very wet, gorgeous Evan King had his hands on each side of me, and he was looking at me like I should have known better than to stay away for so long.

The water was divine, the lighting and atmosphere were flawless. There was a song by Sade called *Paradise* playing loudly through the speakers, and I just stared at Evan, feeling like I was in another dimension. The whole moment was comically perfect.

Without warning, I went under the water. I pushed off of the wall, slipping out of his grasp, and steering myself around Evan. I swam two long strokes underwater before coming up in the middle of the pool. I turned back to look for Evan, but he was already on his way to me. He came up beside me, and I was so surprised that I gasped when he came out of the water. He grabbed onto me, holding me up, focusing on me.

"Are you okay?" he asked, holding onto me.

"Y-yeah, I didn't know you were right behind me."

His arm came around me. His hand was touching my back. He was doing it lightly, but he was touching me—steadying me, holding me up. It was a little deeper where I was standing, and I swam in place, moving my arms and barely tiptoeing. Finally, I held onto his arms. "I had to cool off," I said, repeating what he said earlier.

"Oh, you did? Why's that," he asked, flirting. "Why'd you have to cool off?"

"I don't know. The Sade, and the lights, and the pool... and all that talk about Billy Freeman's party. I had to get away from you for a second."

"At least you didn't have to stop yourself from punching a news man in the mouth," he said.

I laughed and reached for the side of the pool, holding onto the edge. "I did want to punch him a little, that first time he came out because I knew you got the wrong idea about us. I thought I wasn't going to see you again."

"You shouldn't have given up that easily."

"I'm not entirely sure that I would have," I said.

"What do you mean?" he asked.

"I don't know. I thought about trying to call your room or something. I hated that you were here in Corpus and I only got to talk to you for a second."

"I hated that, too. I was already freaking out that I saw you, and then your smell, and then once you walked off, I kept thinking about you wearing that Huskers sweatshirt, and then, I just had to try to find you again."

I put my arms up over the side of the pool, resting my face near the edge as I looked over at Evan. The look in our eyes said it all. We didn't have to speak the words. Both of us were happy and relieved that we connected. We were attracted to each other, and neither of us had significant others.

If only he wasn't leaving in the morning.

CHAPTER 8

I chose not to think about Evan's imminent departure. I would make the most of this night—I would make the most of every moment.

We talked as we swam. Every once in a while, one of us would randomly go under and swim to a different location, surprising the other person. It was always funny timing, and we always chased after the other person when we did it. We talked to each other for a while and then we hooked up with his friends and hung out with them, swimming and judging the boys' dives into the deep end.

Evan and I made all sorts of accidental contact underwater as we swam around, but there was never a time when he pulled me in, holding me in his arms like I thought he might, like I wished he would.

He was a total gentleman. He watched over me, making sure I was comfortable and content. He stayed right next to me, but he only touched me by accident or when necessary. One time, he grabbed onto me to shield me from a particularly large splash from a cannonball performed by Shawn. That moment was amazing and way too fleeting.

We swam for a long while and were some of the only people remaining when it was time for the pool to close. The hotel staff gave us a five-minute warning, and we used that time to get out of the pool.

"What do you guys want to do after this?" Michelle asked, as we gathered on the side to dry off.

"We need to get going," Matt said, sounding no-nonsense. "It's been fun, but we have to be up early in the morning."

Jesse made a noise of protest, but it was fake. He was doing it for the girls' sake—just to be nice.

"I hope you don't have to leave right now," Evan said, leaning over to speak only to me. He towel-dried his hair to shield us from the others.

"I thought you guys needed to get to bed," I whispered, staring straight at him and feeling desperate not to leave his side.

Evan shook his head a little, reassuring me. "That doesn't apply to you."

I gave him a little nod, letting him know I was game for staying as long as he'd have me.

We separated for a few minutes, the boys going one way, and us girls going the other as we went into the changing rooms. The girls didn't want to miss them on the way out, and they made it out of the changing room faster than the guys.

I was the last one dressed, and I had gone fast, so I knew the others were anxious to get out there.

I made it out at the same time as the guys, and we converged in the hall. It was painfully obvious that the ladies still had hope we would all hang out. They stuck close to the guys, and hung onto every word they said.

We walked to the elevator. All of us were headed down. The boys' rooms were on the fifth floor and the girls needed to go to the lobby.

The elevator doors opened, and Matt stuck his hand out to hold it open. "You ladies go first," he said, gesturing for them to get on. "I don't think there's room for all of us, so we'll just wait and take the next one."

The girls got into the elevator, but I stayed where I was. More than one of them gave me a curious look.

"Are you staying?" Michelle asked, obviously thinking I should be with them.

"Yes, Izzy's with me," Evan said. He put a hand in front of me, but I wasn't going anywhere.

Within a couple of minutes, Evan and I said goodnight to Justin and Jesse, and went to the room that Evan was sharing with Matt and Shawn. It was a one-bedroom suite, and Matt went into the bedroom to make a phone call, leaving Evan and me in the main living area with Shawn.

We went to sit on the couch while Shawn went to the small attached kitchen area.

"What do y'all wanna watch?" Shawn asked from the kitchen. He stuck his head into the fridge, and Evan turned to look at him.

"There wasn't anything in there the first three times you looked."

"Bro, why didn't we go to the store?" Shawn asked. "You gotta know you're gonna be hungry after swimming."

Shawn was funny. He was genuinely surprised and disappointed that there was no magical food in the fridge.

"I guess I'm running to the vending machine," he said. He huffed and puffed about it as he was putting on his shoes, but then he smiled and turned around as he got to the door. "What do y'all want?" he asked.

"Just get a couple of snacks," Evan said. "I'll pay you back later."

"I got you," Shawn said nodding like he had everything under control. He hesitated and looked at me on his way out, raising his eyebrows, and smiling at me. "Y'all be good," he said.

That caused my heart to pound. I smiled at Shawn. "*You* be good," I said, since he was nothing but trouble.

Shawn smiled as he closed the door.

Evan adjusted in the corner of the couch, and I turned toward him. We weren't touching, but there was only an inch of space between our legs. He was a big guy, lean but muscular and masculine. I got caught up noticing how perfect his physique was and thinking about how much he had changed since we were younger.

"I'll bet he comes back with five different things," I said.

"Five? Just five?" Evan said, smiling at me. "Try double that. I'll bet he'll spend every bit of twenty bucks."

"In a vending machine?" I asked.

"Yes. Easy."

"How many things will twenty bucks get you?" I asked. I adjusted, sitting sideways and making casual conversation. We had already brought up things like our lack of significant others. We both knew we were attracted to each other. But rather than just sit there and stare at him dramatically or try to make some kind of move, I made easy conversation. "Ten items?"

"Are they two bucks a piece?" he asked.

"I guess it depends on what they have."

"I saw one in the hall with chips and candy bars and all the normal vending stuff," I said.

"He'll spend more than ten dollars for sure."

"That's hilarious," I said, shaking my head. "I've never been friends with a linebacker."

"Yeah, you were. That's what Bobby and Ed McGinnis played."

"Really?" I said, picturing the McGinnis brothers. "I heard Bobby married Bridgette Timmons," I said.

"He did," Evan agreed. "I saw them at the hardware store last time I was in town."

"Yeah, next time I go home, I'll have to stop by the store and see you," I said.

"You better." He said.

He gazed at me, looking me over. I stared at him. Matt was in the other room talking, and Shawn had already turned on the TV, so there was noise. But neither of us paid attention to it. My heart was pounding, and I adjusted again.

"I don't even know where to begin," he said. He spoke slowly and sincerely, staring at me intently.

"Where to begin with what?" I asked.

"With you," he said.

"What about me? We've been together all night. We don't need to begin. We already began."

He shrugged nonchalantly, shaking his head. "If you don't know what I'm saying, then I guess it's never mind," he said.

"What?"

"No. Not never mind. Yes mind. What were you talking about?"

He smiled at my quiet enthusiasm. "I'm talking about you. Me and you. I just want to constantly hold onto you—touch you." Evan spoke with sincerity, but even as he said those words, we were separated by inches of space... feet even.

I shook my head at him. "I never, ever thought you were going to say that," I said, lightheartedly. "That's the last thing I expected you to say just now."

"What? How? What do you mean? That's all I can think about." Evan looked so surprised that I couldn't stop smiling. "I don't even know where to begin," he continued. "It's like you're this fragile, delicate, breakable thing. I don't know how to touch you or where to start."

I looked him over, my heart pounding. "I know you've held plenty of girls' hands, Evan King."

"Never yours," he said.

I shifted again, feeling jittery and restless, shaken. "Mine's the same as any other," I said.

"No, it's really not."

I held up my hand, turning it over as if inspecting it. I let out a little self-deprecating sigh. "I was going to tell you my hand's the same as any other, but it's not even that good. I have a chipped nail right there, and I'm shaking like a leaf on a—" I was about to say "—tree," but Evan reached out and took my hand.

He snatched it out of the air as I was speaking, and I stopped short of the end of my sentence. Evan took my hand, pulling it close to him. He stared at it, inspecting it for a second before slowly turning to me.

"If you thought I was shaking a minute ago..." I said, making fun of myself.

He held my hand with both of his, cradling it, steadying me gently. I felt like I might shatter into a thousand tiny pieces.

"How did I end up here?" Evan said dazedly, reading my mind.

"I was thinking that, too," I said.

"It's God," he said. "There's no other possibility. You even smell like Him."

I had no time to respond to Evan's statement. Shawn came in the door talking and making noise. I flinched a little and I thought Evan might let go of my hand, but he didn't. He held onto me.

"Do you need help?" he asked when we saw Shawn come in the door with his hands full."

"Oh, my goodness," I said when I saw how much food Shawn had in his arms.

"They had microwave popcorn over there," he said. "I'm about to pop that right now. Did y'all find a movie?"

"No, we were waiting on you to do that," Evan said.

"I'm popping popcorn. Do you want some? I got two bags. Do we have a microwave?"

"Did you buy microwave popcorn and not know if we had a microwave?" Evan said, still holding my hand.

"I got some other stuff, too, just in case," Shawn said. "But I see that we do have a microwave anyway, so…"

I adjusted so that I was facing Shawn, and even then, Evan kept a hold of my hand.

"Do you need some help in there?" I offered, talking to Shawn.

"No, ma'am, I don't, I'm just gonna pop this corn and then I'll… well, actually, yeah, I do need help. Y'all need to find a movie. I've got my hands full with food over here. The least y'all could do is find something on the TV."

Evan reached out and grabbed the remote. He sat back and began scrolling through the channels with his right hand, but he didn't let go of me with his left.

This was different than the way we had been acting before. He was blatantly holding my hand, and our hands were resting on his leg.

He had figured out the perfect place to begin.

CHAPTER 9

*E*van and I were sitting on the couch a few minutes later when Shawn came toward us. He had a bag of steaming popcorn and three other snacks in one hand and a soda in the other. He set everything but the popcorn on the coffee table right in front of us and then stood there and stared at us. He smiled and reached into the bag before tossing a piece of popcorn to Evan.

Evan didn't even move. The popcorn just went over his head.

"What are you doing?" Shawn said.

"What am I doing, what are *you* doing? You're the one throwing popcorn."

"Yeah but you're the one *missing* it."

"How was I supposed to catch that one?"

"Jump," Shawn said. I could tell by his expression that he was joking, and by the fact that he had his hand in the bag that he was going to do it again.

He tossed another piece of popcorn into the air, only this time, he caught it with his own mouth. "That's how it's done, son!"

He glanced at Evan with a satisfied smirk and Evan made a playful scoffing noise. "Give me another one, then," Evan said.

Shawn aimed and carefully tossed a piece of popcorn, and Evan caught it easily.

"Okay, I'll try one," I said, even though no one had asked me."

"Ooh, the lady wants to try one," Shawn said excitedly. "That's my girl, let me see, let me see…" He carefully aimed, tossing it where I had the absolute best chance of catching it. It was a great throw, but I just couldn't rope it into my mouth. It hit my lip, near my nose, and bounced onto my lap. I quickly picked it up and popped it into my mouth, chewing and looking at Shawn.

"One more," I said. "Three chances. I have to get one out of three."

"Okay, here we go," Shawn said, looking serious. This one was a little high, and it hit me on my cheek, near my eye. It fell onto my lap and Evan reached across me, picked it up, and ate it.

"Okay last one," I said. "I have to get this one." I sat up. It was the first time I let go of Evan's hand, and I regretted it instantly.

Shawn and I made eye contact and then he held out the popcorn and gently tossed it into the air. It was a perfect throw. I watched it come toward me, moving my mouth under it and praying for a goal. I was expecting it, and still it scared me when it hit my tongue. I caught it! I stashed the popcorn in the side of my mouth when I stood up, raising my arms.

I hugged Shawn who laughed and hugged me back.

"I love this girl," Shawn said.

"No kidding," Evan said. "Who wouldn't?" he reached up and took a hold of my shirt, tugging me to the couch again. I let him pull me off balance, and I teetered and sat clumsily, landing much closer to Evan this time.

Just as I was sitting down, Shawn sat next to us, taking up all of the remaining room on the couch. It wasn't a huge couch. Three regular-sized people would have been tight on it, but Shawn was gigantic and Evan wasn't small.

"What are you doing, you're gonna break it, there's a chair right over there."

Evan and Shawn treated each other like brothers. I had been around them enough this evening to know this was their normal banter.

"I'm not breaking anything. That chair isn't comfortable, and the couch is right in front of the TV. You expect me to sit over there and not be able to see?"

"I don't mind him sitting here," I said since I appreciated being smashed next to Evan. I didn't want Shawn to move. I was closer to Evan now. I wasn't sitting on his lap but I was definitely leaning on him.

Shawn got settled with his popcorn in his lap. Evan adjusted me in his arms, moving and shifting until we were both comfortable.

I was in heaven. He wasn't just holding my hand. He was holding me. I was in Evan King's arms. I had experienced this under very different circumstances the year before.

I had dreamed about it happening like this. I had dreamed about it for years. Even as a little girl I had imagined Evan holding my hand. I relaxed into his arms, feeling like it was the most natural place in the world for me to be.

We sat there for over an hour, watching television and talking to Shawn. Matt came out of the bedroom and announced that he was going to bed. He mentioned that he was setting an alarm for seven o'clock, and Shawn groaned.

I sat up and looked at Evan after Matt left the room. "I need to let you guys get some sleep."

"Take the rest of those Sweetarts," Shawn said.

He bought all that vending machine candy, and it made him happy that I liked it. We had eaten almost a whole roll of Sweetarts together.

"I like you, Izzy Pop," that was Shawn's new nickname for me. He was referring to Iggy Pop, obviously. I was pretty sure he thought Iggy Pop's real name was Izzy Pop. Either way, I didn't mind being called that.

"The pleasure has been entirely all mine, Big Shawn Culpepper."

I said the statement in my newscaster's voice, and Shawn cracked up.

I reached out to squeeze his leg in a gesture of goodbye, and he stood up to hug me. It was funny being squeezed by 290 pounds of man, and I giggled as he lifted me off the floor.

"Bye Shawn," I said when he set me down. "Y'all have fun in Mexico. And goodness, going to Nebraska and graduating after that. Congratulations. You have a big few weeks ahead."

"Yes ma'am, and thank you," Shawn said.

I reached out and touched his arm. I felt nostalgic about saying goodbye to him. He was from North Texas, so we promised we'd see each other again.

Evan told Shawn that he was walking me to my car and that he would be right back. We left the room. Evan held my hand in the hall, but before we got to the elevator door, he stopped and leaned against the wall, pulling me with him, taking me into his arms.

We were so close that I could feel his chest rising and falling as he breathed. He stared down at me, holding me, his arms wrapped securely around me.

"Don't go," he said. Just after he said it, he leaned down and kissed my cheek, right next to my mouth. It was brief and he pulled back, gazing at me as he spoke again.

"I don't want to say goodbye to you, Izzy. What are we going to do?"

"I don't know," I said.

Evan's lips had been on my face, and I was devastated by it—dazed and distracted. It happened so quickly that I hardly had time to appreciate it. I wanted to feel it again. I needed to.

I leaned upward and without hesitation, I placed my lips directly on his. I had no idea where I got the bravery to do it, but the fear of it not happening outweighed my trepidation.

I broke contact too quickly, though. I kissed him and then pulled back. The touch was fleeting, like Evan's kiss had been. His mouth was warm and perfect, and then it was apart from mine too quickly.

"You taste like Sweetarts," he said.

I laughed. It had been a few minutes since I had eaten one, and I didn't have the presence of mind to think of specific things like that when we kissed.

"I didn't think I kissed you long enough for you to tell what I tasted like," I said.

I didn't mean it as a challenge, but Evan took it as one. He pulled me in and kissed me again.

This kiss was different.

Evan opened his mouth, sucking gently on my lower lip. I felt the warm silkiness of the inside of his mouth, and I could have melted right then and there. He gently broke away before doing it again. Once, twice, and then a third time, Evan kissed me. They were gentle kisses and they were fleeting, but his mouth was open to me, and I was so thankful to get the deeper connection. I had been aching for it.

He groaned after a long minute and then pulled me to the elevator. I rode down in his arms, and he held my hand through the hotel lobby. "Where's your car?" he asked, when we got halfway through the lobby.

"Valet."

Evan stopped and let out a defeated sigh. "Oh, really? I didn't think about that."

"Yeah, why?"

"Because I thought you were walking to the parking lot. I was going to go with you and sit with you for a few minutes— tell you goodbye."

I sighed, giving him a sweet smile with an edge of disappointment. "I'm sure you could still sit in my car, but it'll be out there with the valet guys. And plus, you need to get to bed. You're traveling tomorrow."

He stared into my eyes. "Izzy."

"What?"

"This isn't the end, okay? It can't be. I don't know how or what we can work out… you know… with your work and… I just really know I want to see you again. I want to make sure we see each other again."

"Yeah. Me too," I said.

"When?" he asked.

"I'm free as early as tomorrow," I said. "No, I'm just playing, I know you guys have plans. I'm just… I know it might be a little while, but maybe once you get back to Nebraska you can call me. We could at least see what each other is up to over the phone and then try to talk about possible times... we... could... see each othe..."

I trailed off slowly because Evan's eyes were watering. He didn't shed a tear, but his eyes filled with moisture. "What?" I said since he was looking at me seriously.

"I just don't want you to leave. It's definitely God who brought you to me, and I just can't... I don't want to leave you. I'm scared this was all a dream—like I'm going to wake up tomorrow and figure out that none of this happened. I mean... I can't just leave it at *we'll talk on the phone and make plans later*. I want to know the plan. Can we please figure it out?"

"Yes," I said. "We can. How about I meet you in Galveston when you move back? That's just a few weeks away."

"Will you be there the day I get there?" he asked.

"Yes," I said. I started to add that it would really help if it was on a weekend rather than a weekday, but I didn't care. I would make it happen.

"Yes?" Evan said, turning and taking me into his arms. The hotel had a large lobby, and it was late, so no one was close enough to hear what we were saying. It didn't matter. I was in Evan's arms and I could think of nothing else.

"Yes," I said. "I'll meet you in Galveston the day you move back."

"The minute I pull into town," he said.

"Please make it on a weekend," I said. The diehard TV host in me had to get that little request in. "But I don't care," I added. "I'll come. I'll be there whenever."

Evan kissed me. He hugged me, held me, wrapped his arms around me, and kissed me like you see in the movies.

Actually, it was way deeper than the kisses you see in the movies. This was not a kiss that was meant for a hotel lobby. Evan obviously did not care where we were. He kissed me passionately, opening his mouth to me and claiming me. In those earth-shattering seconds, Evan kissed me like he was hungry, greedy, and searching. He pulled me in and his tongue came into my mouth. I opened to him, eager to taste him, to connect with him.

That kiss did it.

I was already in love with Evan, but that kiss—the warm, pulsing rhythm of it—I forgot everything and just gave over to it. For a long minute, in that hotel lobby, Evan kissed me deeply, and nothing else mattered. He moved his hand, holding my head, drawing me close.

Evan couldn't care less that we were in a public place. He was unabashed about connecting with me. I knew I was in love with Evan, but this put me over the top. I would never love another man. I would never be able to kiss another man without comparing it to this moment. Nothing could ever top this.

Finally, after a passion-filled minute, Evan pulled back. He didn't let me go. He held me close, looking down at me. "Izzy."

All he said was my name, so I paused and waited for him to continue. "What?" I asked when he didn't speak again right away. My voice was light and soft. I didn't mean it to come out that way, but I couldn't help it. I felt spent and breathless after that kiss.

"We have to say goodbye."

"I know," I said.

I pulled away a little. I was still in his arms but I leaned back to focus on him. I had always given myself grief about him being younger. I always told myself he was off-limits because he was younger than me. But that feeling had completely gone away.

Evan was so big and manly now that I felt small and protected in his arms. I smiled and leaned up to rub my cheek against his. He knew it was a parting gesture on my end, and he let out a reluctant moan as he pulled back.

"Bye," I said.

"Bye, Izzy Abbott." He pulled me in again and put one last kiss on my cheek. "I'll see you soon, okay?"

CHAPTER 10

Evan

$\mathcal{E}$van was desperately in love with Izabel Abbott. He was crazy about her. It wasn't just infatuation. He was captivated, fascinated, heart-achingly in love. She was serious, but she was funny at the same time, and she cracked him and Shawn up by doing her official interview voice.

Evan had feelings for Izzy a long time ago, and tonight they were unearthed in a crippling way. Tonight, he was bashed over the head with them. His chest hurt when he left her. He almost felt like he couldn't breathe. Evan was accustomed to high-pressure situations, and he normally didn't suffer from anxiety, but leaving Izabel made him all stirred up inside. He could not wait until the next time he saw her. He hoped he could make it that long.

He had been looking forward to this Mexico trip for months, and now he wished it wasn't happening at all.

Izzy caused Evan to have drop-everything thoughts. He wanted to ditch Mexico. He wanted to ditch Nebraska and graduation. Heck, he wanted to ditch Galveston. He felt a strong urge to leave everything in his whole life behind so he could stay in Corpus Christi with this woman.

Evan walked into the room to find Shawn sprawled out on the couch with a blanket and grinning at him from ear to ear. "What?" Evan said after he took off his shoes and noticed that Shawn was still lying there, looking smug.

"*What?* I'll tell you what. You were all over that girl."

"Huh? No, I wasn't."

Shawn laughed hard at that, pushing the covers off of him and sitting up a little. "Son, I've never seen you so much as sit next to a girl, and you were holding onto that one like she was a life raft. I've never seen you do that. Stephanie Singleton came around for months, and you didn't so much as touch her."

"I wasn't dating her," Evan said.

"She thought y'all were."

"We were just friends," Evan said.

He went into the kitchen where he opened one of the remaining snacks. It was a candy bar—a Snickers bar. He ate about half of it in one bite. Evan was anxious about leaving Izzy. He didn't feel right about it. *What if he never saw her again?* He felt sick when he thought about it. *How was he supposed to just leave her and trust that she'd be okay? How was she making it down here in Corpus Christi all alone?*

"Du-u-de," Shawn said, laughing. "You are zoned-out. What happened to you down there?"

Evan took a deep breath and let it out with a sigh. "Izzy," he said. "What a trip that I ran into her over here. I feel like I'm dreaming right now."

"Bro, she is hot, though. I can see why you would want to—"

"No," Evan said, cutting him off. "It's not like that. I mean, she is beautiful, but it's not about that."

"Oh no, big E-King is settling down on us."

"I am," Evan admitted unashamedly as he chewed the rest of the chocolate bar.

***

Evan wasn't able to sleep that night. He took a shower and went to bed, but he couldn't sleep. Matt had already gone to sleep, so Evan just climbed into the second bed.

He looked at the ceiling for most of the night. He replayed the evening with Izzy. He kept thinking of things they said and did.

There was something supernatural about Izzy and it wasn't just her smell. Evan was at home with her. He felt like he knew her more deeply than he did. He hadn't seen her in years, and yet he felt close to her.

Evan only got a few hours' sleep before he heard Matt's alarm go off the next morning.

They spent thirty minutes getting dressed, packed, and ready to go. The restaurant downstairs was serving breakfast, and the guys decided to grab a bite to eat. Matt went to talk to the people at the desk and make sure they were checked out of the room.

"Your friend came back," he said, looking at Evan when he came back and joined them at the table. "Or she never left, I'm not sure. I think she was wearing something different last night."

Evan was already getting to the edge of his seat to stand up by the time Matt finished speaking. "Izzy?" he asked, half-standing and looking at Matt.

Matt nodded casually as he sat in his chair.

"Here?" Evan asked.

"Yes," Matt answered.

"Are you sure it was her?" Evan asked.

"It looked just like her."

"Did you talk to her?"

"No, she is all the way across the lobby. She was talking to someone else."

"Who?"

"I don't know. Some guy. Probably a guy who worked here."

"What in the world?" Evan mumbled as he got to his feet. He didn't ask any more questions or hesitate at all. He just began walking off, heading out of the restaurant and toward the lobby.

He was relieved and excited to hear that Izzy was there.

He walked quickly.

She was indeed standing on the other side of the lobby, talking to a man. They were both standing near the front door, and Evan headed straight for them. The guy was in a suit, looking like he was going to a business meeting.

Izzy turned Evan's way as he grew closer. He had been worried about ten different things—*why was she here in the first place, and why was she talking to this man,* but her face lit up with a smile when she saw Evan, and all his worry melted away.

"Here he is," she said. She bit her lip as she regarded Evan, and he leaned in to hug her. She went to him, hugging him back. "Evan this is Luke. He's a friend of mine from college."

"And beyond," Luke explained, shaking Evan's hand. "We've worked together since then."

"Yeah, that's right. Luke used to work with me at the station."

"That was fun," Luke said. "We'll have to get together some time with Millie and them."

"We will," Izzy agreed, smiling.

"I'll call you sometime," Luke said.

"All right, sounds great," she said, being nice but turning to join Evan.

"Hey, it was nice meeting you, Evan. Izzy was telling me you play for that Nebraska football team. I watched the bowl game this year. Pretty impressive. I remember your name. You were good."

"Thank you," Evan said "It was nice meeting you too." He smiled at the man, but he began to walk off, holding Izzy's hand. He had no idea where he was going except that it was away from Luke. The hotel lobby was huge with room dividers and nooks and crannies, so Evan walked around a corner. He stopped and turned when he and Izzy were mostly alone.

Last night hadn't been a dream, Izzy was here.

"What are you doing here?" he asked, even though he was happy about it.

"I'm sorry," she said. She blinked like she was feeling vulnerable, maybe even afraid of something.

"What, Iz? What happened?"

She was wearing different clothes than the ones she had on when she left. In those seconds before she explained, Evan reached out and touched her arm. He felt an electric feeling in his fingers. He was physically affected by touching her.

"Nothing happened," she assured him. She took a deep breath. "I'm tired, so I'm sorry if I don't get my words out right. I went home after I left here, and I tried to go to sleep, but I just kept... I was up, tossing and turning and thinking, and then I just felt like, goodness, I'm still up, and it's probably almost time for Evan to leave for the boat, and then I just decided to come back over here. So, I haven't slept."

He hugged her, feeling relieved that she was back. He was so happy that she just wanted to come see him. At first, he thought something was the matter.

"I'm happy that you came to see me off. Why don't you come grab breakfast with us?"

"No, no, I just wanted to talk to you alone for a second," she said.

She was nervous—a little breathless and timid.

"Okay, what is it?" Evan asked, assuming she would start talking right then.

She licked her lips, looking like they were dry. She was tired and shaken, and Evan held onto her arms and regarded her with a curious, caring expression. "What is it?" he asked, fearing the worst. Maybe she was married. No, that wasn't possible. He knew she wouldn't lie about something like that. But his mind raced in those seconds.

"It wasn't God," she said, in a breathy voice.

"What?"

"The smell. The blanket."

She paused and let out a sigh. She stared downward, unable to look at him.

"I should've told you sooner. I just was so excited to see you and I didn't want to lose the magic of those moments last night. It's my fault. I really should've said something to begin with. I don't want you to think I was tricking you or anything. I didn't mean for it to turn out like this."

"What are you talking about, Izzy?"

"The blanket. The beach. It wasn't God. It was me. That's why the blanket smelled like me, because it *was* me. I was using it before I put it on you."

Her face contorted just a little and she tried her best to hold back tears, but her eyes filled with them.

"I didn't mean to trick you, and when you told me about it, I didn't know what to say. I wanted you to believe it was God. I didn't want to ruin it by saying it was me. But then last night when I was trying to go to sleep, I just kept worrying about it and being mad at myself for not being honest with you, so I was up till four o'clock. And then I just got dressed again and drove over here. I had to set things straight."

Izabel took a deep breath in and out. She couldn't bear to make eye contact with Evan, and he reached out and tilted her face, using a finger under her chin. She looked his way but not directly at him. She was staring at his chest and neck. Evan tilted her head even more, ducking a little and forcing her to look him in the eyes.

"Iz, look at me."

Their eyes met.

He stared into her gorgeous, blue, watering eyes, thinking they looked like precious jewels. He wanted to own them—to keep them in his treasure chest. He wanted those eyes, and the woman attached to them, to be his.

"Are you telling me that you covered me with that blanket on the beach last year?"

She blinked and swallowed, nodding as if she thought it was bad news.

"And the writing in the sand was—"

"Yes. Me. I'm so sorry."

Again, she was staring at his neck, unable to look at him.

They were quiet for a few seconds as he thought about waking up that morning. He remembered God physically holding him, comforting him that night.

"Izzy look at me," he said.

She did. She seemed so timid that he kept a gentle grasp on her arm.

"Tell me what happened," he said quietly. "Tell me what happened on the beach."

She took an unsteady breath. "I saw you there," she said. "I was in town. I stayed with my aunt because there was a surprise party and I couldn't stay at my parents' house. At first, I thought you were just laying out there, looking at the stars, but then I took a walk, and you were still in the same place, so I went to check on you. It was chilly out, and I had the blanket and everything…" She hesitated, lost in thought. "I tried to wake you up so I could help you into the house. I figured you were staying there, at the Senator's. But there was no budging you. You'd stir, but I couldn't wake you up. I stayed out there with you for a little while, and then I left the blanket. And the note," she added. "I'm so sorry I didn't tell you sooner."

CHAPTER 11

Izabel

"*I*zabel, look at me. Baby, look up. Why would you ever be sorry about something like that? Don't say you're sorry."

"I'm not sorry about what happened, I'm just sorry that you thought it was something else, and I didn't know how to tell you. Even now, I don't know if telling you is the right thing. I keep doubting myself. But I already did, so there it is. I tried to wake you that night, but I couldn't. Then I left the blanket and note. My aunt and uncle live two houses down. I went back later that morning to check on you, but you were gone."

Evan stared at me. "Did I say anything to you?" he asked.

I could feel myself blushing when he asked that. "Yes, but it was unintelligible," I said. "I knew you were distressed about your brother. I heard what happened and I put the pieces together."

Evan was quiet for what must've been about ten seconds but felt more like ten years.

"Are you upset or anything?" I asked nervously.

"Izzy, no, I am just trying to take it all in. This is good news. Don't you see? God is still the one who comforted me that night. He still covered me up and left that message. He just used you to do it, which is even better than doing it Himself."

I shivered as he spoke. I was so relieved that a tear escaped my eye and rolled down my cheek. Evan saw it and he caught it with his thumb before leaning down to kiss me right on that spot. He took me in his arms, adjusting, holding me tightly. I was so relieved and tired that I let out an unsteady breath and wrapped my arms around him, hugging him back.

"Thank you, Evan. I wasn't trying to lie to you last night, I just—"

"I know you weren't. You didn't lie."

I took another deep breath. "I know you have to get going."

"And you're exhausted," he said.

"I know. I need to get some rest."

"Do you need help getting home?" he asked. "I can take a minute and drive you."

"No, no, I'm fine. I live close, and I'm not that tired right this second. I know I'll pass out once I get home, though."

I leaned back and looked at him, focusing on the side of his face. I had been so nervous about talking to him that I was unable to take him in before.

"Are you okay?" I asked "Did you get sleep last night?"

"Not a whole lot, but more than you. I'm okay. I'm more worried about you."

"Don't be," I said. "I'm fine. I'm great. I feel so much better now that we've had this conversation."

"I feel so much better now that I know you were with me a year ago. That night changed everything for me, Izzy. I was in a dark place, and that night on the beach changed things for me."

"I'm so glad to hear that," I said. "I was worried about you, but you looked better that next morning."

"Did you stay there with me all night?" he asked.

There were a few seconds of silence.

"Yes," I said. "At first, I was just trying to get you warm, but then I fell asleep. I thought about you a lot after that. I should've maybe checked in on you, I wanted to, but I didn't know how to tell you what happened. I thought you might want to put it behind you, anyway. I started keeping up with your football team and how good you guys were doing, and I knew you were okay."

"I'm more okay now," he said.

"I know. I can tell that. You look amazing. I'm so happy for—"

"I meant I'm more okay now that you're here. Now that you're in my arms and I'm awake, and you're not just trying to sneak up on me with my eyes closed."

I sighed and smiled, feeling so relieved. I popped up and put a kiss on his cheek. "Thank you."

Evan held me in place, staring straight into my eyes from only a couple of inches away. "Did you... hold onto me... or did I... hold onto you?"

I nodded slowly.

"Thank you," he said. "Things make more sense now, honestly. I know for sure it was both of you—both of you helped me that night. God brought you to me."

We stayed there for a few seconds, lightly embracing in a tucked away section of the lobby before I reluctantly told Evan I needed to let him go.

I knew his friends were waiting on him and that he needed to be going. I was so relieved about his reaction to my news that it made saying goodbye easier.

"I'll call you from Port Isabel to check on you," he said. "I'm not sure what time it will be, so I'll just leave you a message if I can't get through to your phone."

"It doesn't matter what time," I said.

He leaned in and kissed me on the mouth before pulling back with a smile. His kiss lingered for a second or two, but it was all too fleeting especially when I remembered how he kissed me in this lobby last night. My knees got weak just thinking about it.

"Have fun," I said.

"Thank you," he answered. "We will. I'll call you soon."

I went home and slept for four hours. I set my alarm. I didn't want to wake up, but I knew I wouldn't be able to sleep that night otherwise.

I went through the following afternoon in a blurry haze. It was weird, because I was the only one in Corpus Christi who had experienced last night. It wasn't like I could call my friends and talk about how amazing it was that I ran into Evan King. No one knew what had happened between us, and no one knew how unlikely and surreal it was for me to find him and spend an evening with him.

I was delirious from staying up all night, and that combined with the improbability of spending the night with Evan intensified the dreamlike state I was in the following day. He called me that evening and we talked for an hour.

He said it would be a couple of days before he could call me again, which I completely understood since he was going down to Mexico. He said he would call once he got to Nebraska.

He kept his word.

We talked the day he got back to the States.

Then we talked the day after that, and the day after that. We talked every day.

We talked about important, serious, and silly things alike. I kept him informed about my work, telling him stories of things that happened in interviews and with my colleagues. Evan told me all the moves he was making with getting things wrapped up in Nebraska and setting up for his move to Galveston.

A few times, in passing, we did mention the possibility of me moving back home to Galveston, but mostly our conversations revolved around getting to know each other—our likes and dislikes, our goals and philosophies and all the things that made us tick. Evan had a lot going on with wrapping up school and moving, so we didn't use our time making plans that were further in the future.

I already felt like I knew Evan in my heart, but talking to him made me fall more and more in love. We didn't say we loved each other, but I did love him.

It was still early, but I had a hunch we were saving those words for when we saw each other in person. I thought both of us felt like we would spend the rest of our lives together. I wanted it that way, and I truly felt like Evan did as well.

Three weeks passed.

I spoke with Evan on the phone every day, and before I knew it, the time had come for us to finally see each other.

Evan was heading back home to Galveston.

He would be so much closer to me now.

Four hours was nothing.

Evan knew he was in for a lot of packing followed by a long trip. He would be home after 9pm on Friday night, and I would see him the following morning. I would leave Corpus Christi bright and early Saturday morning and drive straight to Galveston and get there before lunch.

That was the plan, anyway.

But I didn't follow it.

I decided to go early.

Evan had no idea.

I recorded a message for my answering machine so he would get it when he called me Friday evening. The message said that I was at my parents' house. I left their number on the recording, knowing that Evan would get in touch with me there after he called my house.

I left Corpus Christi before four o'clock in the afternoon, so I was almost sure I would beat Evan to Galveston. I was so excited that I could hardly contain myself. I had fantasized about the moment when I would see him again.

I was so excited about seeing him that I listened to pop music and sang along during my trip. I was on pins and needles about surprising Evan, and I was glad I would be there early to freshen up and visit with my parents.

There were a lot of backroads on the trip from Corpus Christi to Galveston, and I had my favorite route memorized.

I was driving sixty-eight miles an hour down Highway 288 on the other side of Lake Jackson when it happened. I saw it unfold, but there was no way for me to stop myself in time or change my trajectory.

A semi-truck crossed the center line, and I saw it wobble in a way that looked odd and wrong. I saw it tip over, coming into my lane like a whip, sliding on its side. There was a car between myself and the truck, and I just knew in my heart that I was going to hit them both.

That split second seemed like a helpless eternity.

I hit my breaks and turned the steering wheel abruptly to the side, doing my very best to stop and save myself.

Reflexively, I ducked as I held onto the steering wheel, hiding behind it. The car erupted with a violent shudder as a gigantic piece of metal scraped over my car. In the next second, I felt my surroundings crumple and heard the window shatter. I was thrown into a chaotic whirlwind of shattering glass and twisting metal. The sound was so loud that I could hear nothing. I vaguely had the thought that I would have to fight for my life, and then there was a sensation of tumbling and darkness.

I woke up what must have been seconds later.

I had no idea what brought me back to awareness.

There was smoke and noise, and I was at a dead stop. *Was I stopped?* I glanced out of the window but it was shattered so I could see nothing. It was in a different location, too. And the steering wheel… wait, no, yes, the steering wheel was in my hand and it was somehow not attached to anything else. Or was it? Maybe it was and it was just in a different location now.

I peeled my hands off of it either way. I blinked and tried to find a fixed point in the crumpled confusion of my car. I tried to decide what to do next. Something told me to get out, but I didn't know where to begin. I couldn't figure out where my door handle had gone. I couldn't come up with a better plan than to hoist myself across the passenger's side and get out of that door.

I saw a drop of blood when I turned, and I touched my head to find that it was wet. I looked at my fingers, and there was indeed blood. I got lightheaded for a second when I saw that, but then I thought about Evan.

I had to get out of here. I had to get to him. I began to move again and I caught sight of my bag in the back seat. I absentmindedly thought that I needed that for my trip.

My car might be in bad enough shape that it couldn't to make it to Galveston, so I needed to get that bag. I reached for it, and I felt a sharp pain in my arm. I took a second to stare at it. It didn't look injured, but it certainly hurt. I reached out with the other hand, but I couldn't get to my bag.

It took a long time for me to get into a position where I could get my bag, and then once I got it, I realized I was going to have a hard time going anywhere else. That thought sent a whooshing flood of anxiety through me, and I got close to losing consciousness. I begged myself to stay awake.

And then there was a blinding light.

Someone was there.

"We're here to help you, ma'am. Is there anyone else in the vehicle?"

"No." My voice came out weak and hoarse, and I cleared my throat. "No," I repeated. "I'm alone."

"Okay, just relax and we'll help you out."

"I need to get my bag and get to Galveston. Is my car wrecked too bad to drive it there, you think?"

"Yes, ma'am, I don't think you'll be driving your car tonight."

Looking back on it, I could see that he probably thought it was cute that I would ask such a thing, but at the moment, I thought my car might actually be okay to finish the trip. I was confused. I tried to focus on things, but my mind was racing in a weird way. My ears were stopped up, and I was relatively sure I was speaking too loudly to the nice man who was trying to help me.

"I'm Izabel Abbott from KRSM," I said, trying to lower my volume and sound normal.

"I host Meet Your Neighbor at noon."

I knew, even as I said it, that it was absurd for me to introduce myself, but I just said the first thing that came to my mind.

"I'm glad to meet you Izabel Abbott," he said as he worked to open the door. "Do you know what day it is today?"

"The weekend," I said. "Evan's coming home. He might be home already. What time is it?"

CHAPTER 12

Evan

$\mathcal{J}$he road had grown old after driving straight from Nebraska all the way to the Texas coast. It was a leg-numbingly long trip. It was one Evan had made before, but it never got any shorter. He was hauling a lot of stuff, too. He was a simple guy, but by the time he spent four years in Nebraska, he had accumulated some things.

His dad and his cousin, Will, came to Nebraska with a truck and small covered trailer and help him get moved. Will rode back in Evan's truck so they could hang out. They were the same age and had always been close. Will caught Evan up on everything that had happened with their siblings and cousins and everyone else in Galveston.

Tara, Will's sister, had opened a ballet school on Bank Street. It was next door to the hardware store that Evan's family owned and across the street from the boxing gym that Will's dad owned. The whole block of Bank Street, between 23rd and 24th, had businesses that were run by Evan's friends and family.

"I went into Tara's dance place that last time I was here—after Phillip's funeral," Evan said.

"Oh, yeah, I forgot you saw it," Will said. "Well, she's busy. Her business took off, and she had to hire these… ohhh, dude… there's two new girls working over there, and they're both… Evan, let me just say…. I've been going to the gym every day lately to try to run into this girl."

"Why don't you just go talk to her? Your sister's her boss. Surely, she could introduce you."

"There's two of them," Will said. "One for each of us."

"Will."

"What?"

"What did I tell you?"

"That you're talking to Izzy Abbott."

"So, why would I want to talk to Tara's new employee?"

"Because, Evan, you're not married yet. You're still looking, technically. I know Izzy's hot and everything, but doesn't she live in Corpus Christi? These girls are right here on Bank Street. And they're pretty, just like Izzy. They came from Houston, and they're already trained ballerinas."

"Thanks, but I'll just stick with Izzy," Evan said, grinning at his cousin.

They were having this conversation as they neared the home of Daniel and Abby King. Evan's parents had moved after Phillip died. They bought two acres of property and a nice home that, until now, Evan had only seen in pictures.

"Oh, look at that yard! And I like how this driveway curves," Evan said as they pulled in ahead of his dad.

"Have you seen pictures of the house?" Will asked.

"Yeah, Mom had a bunch of pictures with her at the playoff games, remember?"

"Oh, yeah, that's right. Did you hear who bought your parents' old house?"

"Yeah, your sister," Evan said.

Will nodded dazedly.

They were both exhausted. Evan was tired, but he was in the best mood. He was home, and his lady was meeting him there in the morning. She would come straight to his parent's house when she drove into town. He had already told her to do that.

He felt happy as he rolled into their driveway. It was the first time he felt peaceful and comfortable about coming home. Part of him felt guilty about acknowledging that, but Phillip's absence was like the absence of a dark cloud. Evan had regrets with his brother. He would give anything to have him back. But his Galveston experience would be a lot different without him there—more peaceful.

Evan saw his mom come outside when they pulled up. It was dark out, but there were lights on in front of the house, and she came outside. She was smiling and waving at him, but her smile was more subdued than normal.

She came down the steps and met them in the driveway, going straight to Evan's side of the truck. Abby hugged her son when he got out, feeling relieved and oh so happy to have him home.

She kissed him on the side of the head, even though he was too tall for that now and she had to pull his head down to make it happen.

"I'm so glad you're home. I thought you and Dad might call from Houston when you gassed up. I was hoping you would."

"Why?"

"Because I thought you might want to take a detour to Lake Jackson if I would have caught you on the road. I talked to Courtney Abbott, Izabel's sister. Izabel's fine. She's going to be okay, but there was an accident, and she was in it."

"What? Why'd you say Lake Jackson?" he asked.

"Because that's where it happened. She was on her way here. She's in the hospital over there."

Evan felt an instant burst of panicked energy. He could tell his mom was being serious, but he couldn't process the information.

"She's in the hospital? Izzy is? You're sure? Where?"

"Who?" Daniel asked, getting out of his truck and joining the conversation.

"Izabel Abbott," Abby said. "And yes, I'm sure. She was in an accident. Her sister called me an hour ago. They were headed over there. But don't panic, Evan. She's all right. She's very fortunate. It was a bad accident. I think an eighteen-wheeler crossed into her lane. Her car was totaled. Courtney said Izzy had hurt her arm and that she needed a few stitches, but she's okay other than that. I think they ran tests just for precaution, but everything looks good. Courtney said she'll probably get discharged tonight or tomorrow. She just wanted you to know in case you were expecting her tonight. I told her as far as I knew you didn't expect her till the morning."

"W-uh-I'm going there," Evan said. "I'm not just going to wait till she's discharged."

There was just no other option but to go to wherever Izzy was. He needed to leave immediately.

"My truck needs gas," he said. "And it's all packed."

"Take my truck," Will said. "It's been parked here for two days. I just filled it up before I came over here, too."

"You can always take my car," his mom said. "Why don't you come inside—use the restroom and eat. You can even shower if you want to."

"No. Thank you, but no thank you. I'll use the restroom and maybe grab a bite of food for the road, but I'm going to head out right away. Could you do me a favor, Mom? Could you call the hospital and get directions? I'll be coming in on that highway."

"Three-thirty-two," Daniel chimed in since Evan didn't know the name. "Let's go inside and talk for a second. We'll get you some directions and a snack and get you back on the road."

"I'm not going to be able to stay very long," Evan said.

Ten minutes later, Evan was on the road, headed to Lake Jackson. His parents made him promise to be careful and not drive too quickly in his haste to get to Izabel. He ended up driving his mom's car so that Will wouldn't be without his truck.

What vehicle he drove was of no consequence to Evan. He would have taken off in his own truck, full of things, and stopped for gas. He would've run to Lake Jackson on foot if he had to.

Evan drove down country highways to get there. He didn't even care that he had been on the road for an unspeakable amount of time. This trip was different. He was impatient to get to Izzy, and he sat up in the seat for most of the drive.

Finally, he made it to the hospital. He parked in a parking garage and made his way outside and then into the hospital.

He walked straight up to the lady at the information desk.

"Izzy Abbott. Izabel. Izabel Abbott, please. Tell me where she is, please."

"Yes, sir, is she a patient here?"

"Yes. Can you tell me what room?"

"Just a moment. It's not visiting hours right now, and I'm not sure wh—"

"Oh, no, I'm not a visitor. I'm her... husband. She's waiting for me." The lie came out of Evan's mouth easily since he thought that might be his only ticket in.

"Just a minute, let me check..."

"Oh, she was brought in with the wreck on 288. That was really bad."

"Not Izabel, though," Evan said as more of a statement than a question.

"It looks like she's upstairs in room 338. But you'll need to check in with the nurses sta—"

She didn't bother finishing her sentence because Evan had already said, "Thank you," and was beginning to walk off.

"Mister Abbott this is the shortest way to the elevator!"

Evan turned and changed his direction to the way she was indicating. "Thank you," he said not stopping as he walked past her.

"Sir, you need to check in at the nurses' station!" she called as he walked by.

"Yes ma'am," he called over his shoulder.

Evan rode the elevator to the third floor. He stared at himself in the mirrored walls. His leg twitched nervously, and he let it since he didn't have anything better to do on his way up. The elevator door opened, and there was a sign on the wall that had an arrow pointing to the nurses' station and saying that guests must check-in.

Evan didn't heed any of the warnings.

He went straight toward room 338 to see Izzy for himself. Her room was close to the nurses' station, and Evan had to duck behind a wall one time to avoid being seen by them. But he wasn't taking 'no' for an answer, so he figured he shouldn't encounter anyone who might try to say it to him.

He was nervous when he found the door.

He opened it quietly and peered inside.

CHAPTER 13

Izzy

I was lying there, trying not to doze off. I knew they planned on making me spend the night at the hospital, but I had heard one of the doctors mention that I may be able to be discharged early if my scans and bloodwork came back favorable, which so far, they had.

The doctors and nurses had just left my room, and the last one who went out turned off the light. I knew they expected me to go to sleep, but it was difficult because I wanted to be discharged as quickly as possible. I had already seen my parents, so I knew I would have a ride back to Galveston.

"Izabel?" I heard my name from the door, and I looked that way, seeing light stream in through a crack.

"Yes," I said, focusing on that area intensely. It sounded like a man's voice and I thought it was either my dad or a doctor.

Then suddenly I saw Evan peek around the corner. I reached out for him like a child would reach for a parent, and he came into the room instantly, closing the space between us with three long, silent strides. He collapsed next to my bed, staring at me and treating me with far too much gentleness.

"Evan, my Evan, how did you get here?" I whispered excitedly. I felt like I wanted to cry as I took a hold of him and stared at his worried face. "Don't worry. I'm okay. I'm good. How did you get here, my love?" I didn't expect to call him that, but I was overcome by seeing him there, and the pain medicine was making me feel lovey-dovey.

"Are you okay?" he asked, staring at me.

I nodded, and he leaned in and kissed me ever so gently on the cheek, taking in a deep breath. And then he pulled back, looking at me again. His eyes roamed over my arm, which had a cast.

"It's fractured," I said. I lifted my cast and pointed at it with my right hand. "It's this arm bone, up here next to my wrist. They just finished putting this thing on me a few minutes ago. They were all in here—the bone doctor and his nurses."

Evan's gaze traveled to my face, and up to my head which had a bandage. I had been awake and aware when they put it on earlier, and they had shown me what my stitches looked like in the mirror.

"I got nine stitches," I said. "But they're up by my hairline." I tugged on Evan's arm and leaned toward him. I hadn't seen him in far too long. My heart was already with him, and my body desperately wanted to follow.

"Come here. Come next to me," I whispered in a pleading voice. I'm sure it had something to do with the surreal nature of the evening, but I felt so happy and desperate for him that I leaned into him, reaching for him. I pulled him and scooted over to make room, but Evan resisted, staring down at me.

"You're going to hurt yourself," he said. "You're still hooked up to this IV and everything. I don't even think I'm supposed to be in here."

"I want you next to me," I said. "It's better for me. It'll make me heal faster."

I continued to make room for Evan on my bed as I spoke, and he came to sit next to me, turned to the side with his legs hanging off the bed. He sat facing me, leaning over me, holding my hand.

"Come lay by me," I said, wanting him, wanting to hold onto him.

"I will," he promised. "I just want to talk to you for a minute—to look at you. Tell me about what happened to you. What were you doing way over here?"

"I was trying to come in early."

Evan made a face like it pained him to think of me getting into a wreck while doing something for him.

"It wasn't my driving," I said. "It was a freak accident. I was just driving down the road, and the next thing I knew, a truck crossed over and flipped. I tried to get out of the way fast enough, but I just couldn't. A piece of the trailer kind of went over my car, I think. I don't remember it. The cops were explaining it to me earlier."

"How long have you been here?" he asked.

I stared at him because I had no idea. "My parents and Courtney were in here about an hour ago, before the ortho crew came in. I'm not sure how long I've been here. I did scans and everything."

"Are your parents and Courtney still here?"

"Mom and Courtney went back home, but dad said he was staying. I think he went to get something to eat, and maybe now he's in the waiting room. I'm not sure."

"Is he staying the night in here, in your room?"

"I don't know. I hadn't thought of it. I assume he'll be in the waiting room or in here with me, if they don't let me go right away. I don't know where he is right now, actually. I do think he's staying here until I'm done, though."

Evan adjusted, sitting further on the bed, leaning over me. He put his hand on the other side of me, propping himself up. He leaned in and I rested my head on the pillow, looking up at him and feeling like everything was going to be all right now that he was here. "I'm so happy to see you, Evan," I said the words as I touched his arm. "I've been counting the minutes till I see you."

I reached out for him, and he came in for the hug. We wrapped our arms carefully around each other, and for a long time, I just stayed there with Evan, sitting on the bed and hugging. I felt safe and secure in his protective embrace.

"Thank you for coming here," I said finally. Evan held me with an impossible mix of relentlessness and gentleness.

"I got here as soon as I could," he said. "I love you, Izzy. I need you to know that. I'm sorry I haven't said it to you yet. I thought about that the whole way here. I should have learned by now that you need to tell people things... I love you. I want you to be sure of that, because I do."

"I love you, too," I promised him.

He collapsed onto me, and I held onto him, feeling so relieved I could cry. I did cry. We hugged each other for what must have been five minutes. I was sitting straight up and I was so comfortable that I cried and then I almost dozed off in his arms.

"I am so relieved right now," Evan said finally, bringing me to reality.

I turned and motioned to the empty space in the bed next to me. "Please," I said, begging him to lie next to me.

Evan complied, kicking off his shoes before swiveling and stretching out next to me. He was so very gentle, but I wasn't in pain, and I curled up next to him, relishing the feel of his warm body next to me. I had been missing him so much during these last few weeks.

With our current surroundings being sterile like they were, I couldn't necessarily pay attention to Evan's muscular athletic body under only a thin layer of t-shirt. It was a good thing I couldn't, because it was extremely distracting and exciting even in my dazed state. I put my hand on his chest, feeling in love… like I was in a movie scene.

I pictured cotton candy instinctually, and then I focused again on Evan, telling myself that it was okay to get all worked up on the inside since he wouldn't know.

"I am totally normal right now," I said.

I didn't even realize I said my thoughts until Evan laughed at me. He leaned in and kissed my forehead.

I picked my head up and peered over him, making sure he had enough room. The bed was at least as wide as a twin bed, so I knew there was room for both of us.

"Are you hanging off?" I asked, reaching over and feeling the other side of him. I used my cast-covered arm to do it, and Evan froze in place and looked at me.

"What are you doing?"

"I'm checking to see if you're hanging off."

"No, I'm not. I have plenty of room." He sunk into the bed, and I curled up beside him, holding onto him, laying my head on his shoulder.

"I want to stay like this forever," I said.

"You can," he said.

"I can? We are?"

"Yes."

"How when we do that?" I asked.

I was aware that I had misspoken but I was too tired to correct myself.

"How or when will we do it?" he asked.

"Both," I said.

"Well, we can stay like this right now, but also tomorrow. Assuming you get to go home, we can just make you a place on the couch and stay like this. I have some unpacking to do, but I'll be able to be with you most of the day."

"I don't need to lay in bed," I said. "I can help you unpack." I thought of my arm being in a cast when I said that. "Well maybe some light stuff," I added. "But I don't need to stay in bed all day. I'll be fine. What am I supposed to do with this thing for work, though?"

"How long did they say you'll have it?" he asked.

"This one's only on for a few days. They said they'd re-x-ray and decide how long the next one needed to be on. It's just a fracture, though."

"Did you tell them you don't live here?"

I took a second to recall giving the nurse my information when I got there. I relaxed on his chest, speaking dazedly as I responded. "Yeah, they knew. They said I could follow up at home. They told me to go to an orthopedic place in Corpus Christi—they gave me a doctor's name in my paperwork."

Nurses came in a little while later, and eventually my father did, too. They were all surprised to find Evan in my room. Evan insisted on sitting beside me rather than on my bed while others were in the room, but I made it clear that I wanted him there, so he didn't leave.

My dad had followed Evan playing football, and he also knew that I had been talking to him seriously for the last few weeks and that he was the reason I was coming to Galveston this weekend. He wasn't thrown off by Evan being there.

The two gentlemen talked it out and decided that Evan was going to stay in Lake Jackson and let my dad get back to my mother and his own bed. They got along great and both just seemed thankful that my prognosis was good. I felt protected and cared for with Evan there. I fell asleep with him sitting on my bed next to me.

CHAPTER 14

I checked out of the hospital at 6am the following morning. We made the trip back to Galveston, and Evan dropped me off at my parents' house where I slept for most of the day. He came over that night, but I was still a little zonked, so he only stayed for an hour or so.

It was the following morning when I woke up feeling like a human again. I was now on a very minimal amount of ibuprofen and the other stuff had finally worn off, so I was fully awake and alert for the first time since the accident.

It was Sunday, and I called Evan that morning at his parents' house. It was 9am, and I knew they went to church, so I wasn't sure if they'd pick up.

"Hello?" said a woman's voice.

"Hey, Ms. Abby, this is Izabel Abbott."

"Hey, Izabel, how are you doing? I heard all about your accident from Evan. I'm not my mom, though. I'm Lucy."

"Oh, hey, Lucy, I didn't know you were in town."

"My children wore me down once they knew Uncle Evan was coming home this weekend. Mac just finished school, and I just finished a book, so it was good timing."

"Oh, nice, did your husband get to come?"

"No, just me and the kids. We're just staying a couple of nights. We were hoping to get to see you. Evan's all excited to be talking to you again."

I should've done a better job at taking that compliment, but my brain was already on a different path. I was thinking about complimenting her books, and I unintentionally blew past her statement and said, "My little niece loves your books. Courtney's daughter. She has all of them. She keeps begging Courtney to buy her a hedgehog. We keep trying to tell her they don't talk in real life."

"Or do they?" Lucy said in a dramatic tone, joking and causing us both to laugh. "I hope I'm going to get to see you, Izzy," she continued.

"Me too. I was going to talk to Evan to see if he's up for company after church. That's why I was calling."

"Company? You mean you? You're not company. And of course he's up for it. I don't even need to ask Evan. He wants you here. But here he is. He just walked in. Hang on, let me let you talk to him…"

"Bye, Lucy."

"Bye, Izzy, see you later today."

There was rustling and then I heard Evan's voice.

"Hello?"

Even hearing his voice made me giddy. "Hey," I said, smiling. "I'm sorry I fell asleep when you were here yesterday."

"Don't be sorry," he said. "You needed the rest."

"I feel so much better today," I said.

"Do you? I hear it in your voice."

"Yeah, I woke up feeling good. I can't believe all that happened. Where did the weekend go? I'm supposed to be at work tomorrow."

"I hope you're not going to work," he said.

"I'm not. Not tomorrow. I'm taking Monday off. I talked to the station and let them know I'd be back on Tuesday. We have to cancel Monday's show, but I have some things recorded."

"Good," he said.

"I could really head back today, feeling like this, but I didn't want to miss all my time with you. I'll just head back tomorrow instead."

"That's what I'm talking about," he said playfully. "When are you coming over? Do you want me to pick you up for church?"

I glanced at the clock. "What time? I need thirty minutes to get dressed in the state I'm in. I'd love forty-five."

"I'll be at your house in forty-five minutes," he said.

"Does that make you late for church?" I asked.

"I don't know, not much, but it doesn't matter," he said. "Let's do this. I'll be there in forty-five minutes."

I could tell he was excited to see me. His enthusiasm was so obvious that I could hear it over the phone.

I smiled. "Okay, see you in a little while."

I jogged into my old bedroom to look for something to wear. I had my bag from home, and I went straight to that.

It felt so good to take a shower. I had to avoid my cast, but that problem was easily solved with a trash bag and some duct tape. The process of washing and drying my hair was not nearly as easy with stitches and a cast. But I was careful, and the cast was on my left arm, so it wasn't that big of a deal.

I stood in the mirror after getting dressed in a little sundress. I turned to the side, looking at myself with the cast. I wouldn't call the cast a fashionable accessory, but it wasn't terrible to look at. I had the presence of mind to choose light grey as a color, I had a lot of outfits that could blend with grey, and I chose that color with my job in mind.

I was happy with the color once I saw it next to that floral sundress. I wore some black strappy sandals that I had in my closet from years ago. They looked nice with the dress and I felt as comfortable as I could in the whole outfit. I put on some makeup, and I was easily able to avoid the stitches on my forehead.

I styled my hair in a barrette with hair loosely covering the wounded area so that it wouldn't show. It had been bandaged for two days. I would cover it again this evening, but I knew it was fine to let it breathe today. The doctors had told me that.

The whole process of showering took so long that I was still getting dressed when Evan came over. I was in the bathroom and I heard him come in and start talking to my parents.

I tried to wrap things up as quickly as possible, but I still needed to apply mascara. I was just finishing up when my mom peeked into the bathroom.

"Evan's here," she said with wide eyes.

"I heard. I'm almost done. Send him back here, please."

She gave me a nod and then disappeared, and thirty seconds later, I heard footsteps. I was looking at the door when he came around the corner.

"What? What's this? Where's your bandage? You look amazing..."

Evan didn't stop in the doorway like I thought he might. I was still holding the mascara wand in my right hand when he came into the bathroom and took me into his arms. I laughed quietly as he hugged me and then I settled in next to him when he pulled back.

"You look drop... (lean in and kiss on the mouth) dead... (kisssssss) gorgeous."

Evan kissed me four or five times after that, and I eagerly kissed him back, smiling between each one. The feel of his mouth on mine was too much. It gave me fluttering sensations in all sorts of places.

"You seem so much better," he said, holding me tighter than he did yesterday or the day before.

"I am better," I said, hugging him back. "That haze was gone when I woke up this morning, thank goodness."

He kissed me again. He was like the leading man in a movie. This whole situation was surreal. I had wanted Evan for so long that it was both natural and unbelievable that I was standing there in his arms.

"Are you almost ready?" he asked, glancing around.

"Yes. Let me put this thing up, hang on, I don't want to get it on your shirt."

I shifted and screwed the top back onto the tube of mascara, and then I turned to him again and kissed his cheek.

"Hi," I said. "I feel sort of like I'm just seeing you for the first time."

Evan stared at me. He opened his mouth and then closed it again. He was being thoughtful, and I had no idea what he would say.

"Stay alive," he said quietly, slowly. "Izabel, just promise me you will stay alive."

I hadn't been expecting him to say that so I let out a little chuckle. "I promise I will as long as I can."

"Just make sure to do it, okay?" He leaned down and gently rubbed his face next to mine, being so very gentle.

"Okay," I whispered, holding onto him and feeling like I was in heaven. "I'll do my best," I said.

We left right away and went to church with his family. I sat next to his sister, Lucy, who I also knew from school. She was older than me, and I always thought she was so cool. She had a son named Mac when we were in high school. He was 10 years old now. Her daughter, Katie, was five, and her son, Andrew, was four. I knew all of this from talking to Evan during the last month. The kids were nowhere to be found when we arrived and found his family, so I assumed they were in children's church.

Evan reached over and held my hand during the service. He never lost contact with me on the way out, either. We encountered some of his other family—cousins and aunts and uncles and even friends. I knew he had a big family, but I had no idea they all went to the same church. Maybe they didn't. Maybe this wasn't all of them. Maybe it just seemed overwhelming because it was Evan's first weekend back and the entire church was anxious to see him.

A few people recognized me in Galveston, but they remembered me from high school. Most people had no idea I was on a news station now. Evan, however, was a local celebrity. His football team had been completely dominant this year, and everyone in town had been following them. I knew because my father knew I liked Evan and kept me posted about how people in Galveston reacted to him.

I wasn't quite prepared for the onslaught of anxious fans at church, but at the same time, I was fine with it. Evan kept me close, always checking in with me to make sure I was okay.

We stayed after church for about fifteen minutes, talking to a few different groups of people. Evan's family was planning on getting together at Tess and Billy's for lunch. We did some switching-around of vehicles and we added three more to Evan's truck. Ten-year-old Mac and his friend Theo, along with Lucy.

The boys sat in the smaller back cab of Evan's truck, and Lucy sat in the front with us. We talked about my broken arm for a minute and then she asked about my work.

Evan had to stop by the house to pick up something for his mom, and he and the boys went in while I stayed in the truck with Lucy.

"That little boy, Theo, is all the stuff over there in Houston."

"How so?" I asked, thinking she might be joking since he was just a kid.

"Football," she said seriously. "He's only twelve, but you know how Texans get about their football—he's *big time* over there." She acted overly dramatic to be funny, so we were laughing as she added, "No, he's a good little athlete, though. Mac was so excited that he wanted to come on this trip. That's when it pays to have a famous Uncle."

I looked at her, and she smiled and gestured with a flick of her chin to her brother, who was walking with Theo and Mac into the house. Evan was smiling and talking to the boys, and I felt so proud of him.

CHAPTER 15

$\mathcal{I}$f there was one thing I could do, it was feign confidence. I had to do it all the time with my work. It was a huge part of my life. I had to psyche myself up every day to interview people and feel confident in the decisions I made minute-by-minute during unscripted segments of my interviews. I was used to thinking on my feet.

But being around Evan's family was an entirely new beast. I was way too nervous around them. I wanted to impress them. I was in the truck with Lucy while we waited for the guys who had just run into the house. Lucy was a famous writer who had books in Barnes and Noble and a cartoon series.

On a normal day, I would have been able to interview someone in her position. I had interviewed other famous people and done fine. But I cared so deeply about Evan that I wanted to make only the best impression on his family.

"Evan said he was serious about you," Lucy said.

"What?" I asked, in a lighthearted tone, thinking I must have misheard her. I didn't expect her to be so frank.

"My brother," she said. "He told us you were the one."

"Oh, my goodness. Are you serious?" I said, covering my mouth as I let out a little nervous laugh.

"Why?" she asked. "What do you feel about him? Do you not feel the same way? I know you live in Corpus Christi, and he was talking about your job, saying that meant a lot to you. And I knew he was a little younger than you, and you used to date Michael Ellerby."

She sounded a little doubtful, like she hoped I could be devoted to her brother.

I blinked at her. "Lucy, I'm so in love with your brother," I said. "I am, there's no, you shouldn't worry about me. There's no Michael Ellerby, and quite frankly there could be no KRSM. I'd leave anything for your brother."

I regarded Lucy, staring at her sincerely from right next to her in the truck. "Well, I know he wouldn't want you to leave your work," she said taking a deep breath. "He knows you love it and he's really proud of you. I just didn't know how you would make things work because Evan was talking long-term when he mentioned you last night."

"I love your brother," I said, knowing that was going to have to be enough for now. "I think both of us took this car accident as a wake-up call. We've seen each other a little since the accident, but I was still out of it, so we haven't had time to talk."

She shook her head almost imperceptibly, "I've never seen him do that where he just speaks openly to us about a woman and his plans and everything."

"What plans?" I asked.

"Marriage, kids, the whole nine yards," she said. "He was telling our mom she's gonna have more grandbabies."

We both laughed. She at her brother, and me because I was nervous and excited and couldn't believe she was saying any of this.

Lucy looked toward the house which caused me to glance that way. I noticed that the boys were coming.

"Don't tell my brother I told you all that," she said.

"I won't, but is it true?" I asked, needing to hear it again.

She nodded at me with wide eyes and a serious expression. "He's so in love. That's the only reason I brought it up to you. I usually don't interfere in my brother's life or decisions."

We were watching the guys approach as we talked. They were getting closer and would soon come inside the truck. "Well, you don't have to worry about me," I said, speaking quickly and drawing our conversation to an end. "I'm all in."

She breathed a sigh. "You have no idea how relieved I am to hear that."

I smiled at her as the boys opened the door, but in my head, I was thinking how backward it felt that Lucy should be relieved when I was the one who was relieved. I didn't say as much. I just sat there.

Evan was holding a covered dish, and he set it on the floorboard of the back seat.

"Y'all get in the other side!" Lucy yelled, seeing the boys hesitate in the yard near the truck.

"Hang on, I told them I'd throw a couple of passes before we go to Aunt Tess's."

Evan had a football in the back of his truck, and he swapped the covered dish for it. He turned and lifted the football up and held it in that stance that made it look like he was about to throw.

I watched the boys take off sprinting, and then Evan's body shifted just the right way where he was about to let the ball fly in a perfect arching spiral through the air. He wasn't a quarterback, but he looked like one right then. He was confident and comfortable with a football, and he smiled as it flew through the air and Theo caught it and ran for what would be a touchdown.

Mac was right on his tail and he almost took Theo down, which left both boys laughing.

Evan looked into the truck, smiling at us. "One more," he said to his sister.

She didn't protest, and Evan took a couple of steps away from the truck, holding his hand out for Theo to throw it to him. Theo was standing far off, so although his throw was accurate in direction, he was short by about ten feet.

I watched Evan run up to it just in time to scoop it up.

Theo cheered at his ball being caught.

"All right, Mac," Evan said. He got into position, aiming for his nephew who had taken off running to the left. Evan launched the ball, and I watched as it spiraled through the air. That kid, Theo, was older and bigger than Mac, and he was extremely athletic. It would be difficult for Mac to catch the ball with Theo guarding him. But Mac rose to the challenge.

Evan placed the ball where Mac could just barely get to it, and I watched as he reached out and grabbed it with his fingertips.

"Ohhhhhhh!" Evan erupted, jumping and laughing and running toward Mac, who turned and ran a victory lap with the ball. He circled around, grinning from ear to ear as he sprinted back toward us with Theo on his tail.

"Okay, let's go!" Evan called. "We'll throw some more after lunch."

Evan closed the boys into the small backseat before climbing into the driver's seat. I could hear the boys talking and laughing about Mac catching that pass, and I smiled to myself.

"We've been waiting for Uncle Evan to get home, huh?" Lucy said, looking over the seat at the boys.

"Yes maaaa'aaaam!" Mac said excitedly. He was adorable, dark-haired, and constantly ruddy-cheeked from running around. "I'm gonna play for Nebraska when I get in college," Mac said.

"I'm gonna play for UT," Theo said. "My dad's already talking to coaches over there."

Evan glanced at his sister who nodded in confirmation. "His older brother plays for UT Austin," she explained.

"My dad knows about Evan King and about y'all's uncle," Theo said. "Billy Easy or something like that. A boxer."

"Easy Billy," Mac said laughing.

"For real? I thought it was Billy-Easy—I thought Easy was his last name."

Mac laughed at the thought.

"Billy Castro," Evan said. "Castro is his last name. Easy is just a nickname."

"My dad said he used to be the champ."

"He was," Evan said. "And it hasn't been that long since he retired. He could definitely still fight right now. He could beat me up, that's for sure."

Theo giggled at that. "Do you ever even do any boxing?" Theo asked.

"Me?" Mac asked.

"No, I know you do. I saw those punchin' bags in your garage."

"You mean me?" Evan asked.

"Yes, sir."

"I used to, when I lived here before. I'll probably start up again, now that I'm back. I don't want to do it competitively like my uncle if that's what you're asking."

"Then why else would you do it?" Theo asked.

"Self-defense," Lucy said.

"And exercise," Evan said.

"You don't need exercise!" Theo said. "You're already bigger than both of my brothers."

"Yeah, but if I don't keep exercising, I'll lose it."

"Yeah, you got to keep *lifting weights*, every… single… day, huh, Uncle Evan?" Mac was a passionate little boy, and I always smiled when he was around.

"I take a couple days a week off, but yeah, you have to keep in shape if you want to compete because you got freshmen and sophomores coming up, trying to take your spot—just like you two will be going up, starting in high school and then college. You have to train hard all the time so you're ready when something comes open."

"That's how I got my job," I agreed.

"How?" Lucy asked.

"I was working at the news station, and I had to fill in for the lady who used to host that segment. She was good, but the producers… they said… they wanted me to continue with the segment after I filled in for her. That was just how it worked out."

"Did she get mad at you?" Mac asked.

I took a deep breath, thinking about how to answer that. "She… took it well," I said, not mentioning the passive-aggressive behaviors I had to deal with from her and others at the network. "But moving up in the world isn't always easy. Even if she would have made it difficult for me, it wouldn't have been fun, but I still would have taken the job. That other lady still got to keep her job, she just hosts a different segment now."

"Do something," Lucy said.

She was talking to me. She was sitting right next to me, looking at me. I couldn't understand what she meant, so I gave her a curious expression.

"Do one of your questions. Show me how you work. Interview me."

Mac giggled expectantly from the backseat, and I sat up straight, tucking my cast into my lap and turning to face Lucy.

"Good afternoon, Galveston, and welcome to Meet Your Neighbor. I have an exciting guest for you today, Mrs. Lucy Klein, author of the beloved children's book series, Garden City Hedgehogs. (More giggling by Mac and Theo. I wasn't sure if that was the exact name of the series, but I knew I was close, so I went with it.) Welcome, Lucy."

"Thank you, thank you so much," Lucy said in an overly fancy voice. She was in character when she thanked me, but then her face changed, relaxed, as she smiled and widened her eyes. "Whoa, Izzy, that was awesome! Your whole voice and tone and demeanor totally changed. You're a real news lady. That's amazing. I felt like I was on TV just now."

The boys were laughing and commenting from the backseat on my newscaster voice.

"I amped it up for you guys," I said. "But that's about what I sound like on the air." The boys got such a kick out of my newscaster voice that Mac tried imitating me.

"And, yeees," he said in a deep, dignified tone. "I'd like to know more about your hedgehog books that you write…" He was continuing the interview with his mother, and it cracked me up.

I glanced at Lucy who laughed and shook her head at her son. Evan reached out to touch me as he drove. My left arm was awkward because of the cast, so I moved it out of the way and held onto him with my right hand.

"Yes sir, I wrote a lot of them," Lucy said, answering Mac and causing the boys to laugh.

"Did you ever meet anybody famous?" Theo asked.

"Me?" I asked.

"Yes ma'am."

"I did. I met a lot of people who are sort of famous, and a few who were really famous."

"I wish I could meet somebody famous," Theo said.

"You're in the truck with two famous people right now," I said. "Evan and Lucy are both famous, and their Uncle Billy is super famous. He's one of the most famous people I've ever met."

CHAPTER 16

*J*ess and Billy lived in a cool old Victorian home on Bank Street. I knew where Billy Castro lived, but I had never been inside the house before.

A lot of people came over. It was fairly common for them to get together after church on a Sunday, but Evan warned me that there would be even more people than usual since it was his first weekend back in town.

I never counted, but it felt like there were fifty people in that house when we arrived. I met aunts, uncles, cousins, and friends. I recognized most of them from growing up in Galveston, but it had been a long time since I had seen any of them.

Billy was a champion boxer, so I would've never dreamed this would be the case, but he did most of the cooking. He barbequed, and he did a lot of the other kitchen duties, too. Evan's mom, Abby, and her sister, Tess, were in the kitchen most of the time, helping Billy with timing the food and making conversation with any and all who came into the kitchen.

We were in there talking with them for a while before Mac and Theo couldn't take it any longer. I was standing next to Evan when Mac came up to him holding a football and wearing a pleading expression. He got close to us, staring up at his uncle Evan.

"Please can we go throw some passes?" he asked.

Evan didn't answer, he just glanced across the room. "Uncle Billy, how much longer on lunch?"

"Four minutes," Billy answered in a matter-of-fact tone as he carried a tray of meat across the kitchen to set on a trivet on the counter.

Evan leaned down to talk to Mac. "Let's wait four minutes, since we're about to eat. I'll take you and Theo, and Will, Josh, Trey, and whoever else wants to go, back to Pap and Nana's after this and we can get a nice game in."

"Yessss!" Mac said jumping.

"Yeah, it's crowded over here with all the cars parked on the street," Lucy said. "If you and Theo go back outside, I want you to stay in the yard."

"Yes, ma'am!" he said, taking off to go give Theo the good news.

"And come back in a minute. You heard Uncle Billy. We're about to eat." She turned and glanced at Evan. "Thank you. They're going to love that."

"Who's going to love what?" Will asked, coming up from behind us. On his way around, he smacked Mac on the rear end, causing the boy to wiggle out of the way, laughing.

"I told Mac and Theo I would play a quick football game with them after lunch," Evan said. "I know we can get Josh to play, and Trey, but who else? We need a couple of extra guys. I can get my dad to play, especially if we do it at our house," he added.

"I could call a few people, Jacob and them, to come meet us at your house," Will said. "I'm up for whatever."

"Yeah, that sounds good," Evan said.

"All right. I'll go call Jacob."

"Tell them to meet us at two-thirty," Evan said.

Will smiled and nodded as he walked away.

"Thank you, guys!" Lucy said, hearing everything. "Mac and Theo are gonna be so excited to play with the big boys."

Just after she said that, Tara whisked me away to go tour her mother's studio space before we ate lunch. Billy's wife, Tess, was a painter who was well-known in the area for her lighthearted, chunky, beach-themed paintings. My mom was a fan of hers, and we had an original and two prints in our house.

The truth was, if I wasn't so out of my mind with love and excitement over Evan, I would be starstruck and nervous in front of all of these people. But I was so hyped about Evan that all of the emotions sort of canceled themselves out and I was left feeling neutral and comfortable.

I talked to Tara about her mom's art and about her ballet studio. She and her husband, Trey, had an eight-month-old baby boy, William Rhys Harper. William was Tara's father's name, but it was also Trey's real name. Their son was the fifth William in the family, and because of that, he got called Nickel. Someone had started it on account of a nickel being worth five cents, and then it just stuck.

Nickel was on Tara's hip the whole time, so he came with us on the quick studio tour.

We got back just in time to bless the food. Billy called us into the kitchen.

"All right, I just wanted to thank everybody for coming. We're obviously excited to have Evan back home with us, and Miss Izabel, his friend, welcome, to you. We're so glad that you're okay after your accident." (Everyone turned and looked at me when he said my name, and Evan came to stand behind me, pulling me next to him.)

"Thank you," I said to Billy, feeling a little shy.

He smiled and thankfully went right on talking. "Lucy's here with Mac and the kids, but we're missing Drew."

"He's working on a big case," Abby announced on her son-in-law's behalf.

"Okay, well, let's keep Drew's big case in our prayers." He clasped his hands in front of him. "Father, thank you for family. Thank you for this day that we can all take a break from all the things we do all week and make some time to get together and enjoy each other's company. Thank you for this food, thank you that we never go hungry. Please bless this food, may it nourish our bodies. Amen."

He looked up.

"All right, let's serve ourselves. Go ahead and get stuffed with barbeque, and then we can break into Aunt Abby's cookies."

"I've already had three of them!" Mac announced, telling on himself.

Will was standing near Mac, and he reached over and captured him, trying to tickle Mac as he squirmed and giggled.

People were already talking amongst themselves and beginning to get in line for the buffet. It was suddenly chaotic in there, and Evan steadied me in his arms, pulling me close. There was no mistaking the PDA. He wasn't overboard with it, but I was not just Evan's friend, and he made that apparent.

Abby came up to us. "Did you get to see Tess's art room?"

"Oh, yes ma'am," I said. "I could live in there."

"I know, isn't that window the best?"

"Yes, and to have her work space set up with that light and that view. Such inspiration."

"I know," Abby said. "I try to go up there and have coffee with her while she paints. Sometimes we just sit quietly, listening to music or just the sounds of the city. She'll paint, and I'll just watch her or stare out of the window."

"I bet that's lovely," I said.

"It is," Abby agreed. "You have sisters. Are you close to them?"

I nodded. "I'm the youngest by six years, so we're not too close in age, but we're close, yes ma'am."

We ate and visited with his family for the next hour, and Evan almost never strayed from my side. He was always glancing at me to make sure I was comfortable and happy.

He stood next to me on his uncle's front porch. Billy and Tess didn't have a big yard, but there was still a game of catch going on. Several people were sitting out there with us, and Evan spoke quietly when he turned to me and said, "I need to go to my parents' house to change clothes. We should head out now before everyone else comes over."

"Oh, okay, are you ready to go?"

"Yeah."

I could tell he was kind of being quiet about it which made me think he wanted us to have some privacy. My heart began to race. Privacy with Evan would be an ideal scenario for me. I had seen him alone since my accident, but never when I felt like myself.

But today, I felt more like myself than ever, and I was aching for him, aching to stare at him with no one else around, aching to kiss him.

He pulled me inside the house, and we grabbed our things. I could tell he wanted a second alone with me as much as I wanted it with him. The air between us was charged. We told his parents what we were doing and said goodbye to the ones who were inside, but we made a quiet exit.

We were in the driveway, about to get in his truck, when Mac and Theo came running up to us. "Where you goin'?" Mac asked.

"To Pap and Nana's to change and get ready for y'all," Evan said.

"Oh, no, don't worry, me and Theo will just ride with you right now!" Mac turned toward the house. "Hey, Mom!"

"Yeah?"

"We're going back to Pap and Nana's with Uncle Evan. We need to change and get ready for the big game."

"Okay!" Lucy called as she chased after the younger ones.

"She said okay," Mac said looking at Evan excitedly, as if that was the only thing holding us back.

"Great," I said, seeing how precious he was.

"Yesss, I love Evan's truck," Theo said. "Hey, you got a system in here?"

Evan looked at Theo seriously as the boy climbed into the back seat. He was deadpan when he said, "Son, do you think I would actually have a truck without a system? What kind of man do you think I am?"

Both boys laughed with delight at Evan, and they went straight to talking about what songs they wanted to hear. Evan passed them the CD case to shuffle through while he got the truck started.

"Sorry," he mouthed to me where his nephew couldn't hear.

I wanted to answer him back, but I was afraid they could hear me so I said "I'm glad you guys rode with us."

"I know, me too," Theo said. "Your Uncle Will said he had like five friends coming to play. We gotta get ready for 'em."

CHAPTER 17

*L*ucy, Tara, and their cousin, Jenny got in on the game
of football. I would have normally done the same, but
I wasn't about to in my current condition. It was touch football,
and no one would try to hurt me, but there was still running
and tripping and falling, and I just couldn't manage that two
days after a car accident. I thought it was cool that the girls
played, though, and I definitely would have joined them under
different circumstances.

As it stood, I sat on the porch with Abby and her sister-in-
law, Laney.

I could not take my eyes off of Evan. I tried to watch other
people, and for a few seconds at a time, I was able to do it, but
my eyes kept roaming back to Evan. He played quarterback
at first, and then Will wanted to switch, so Evan caught some
passes. It was the same athleticism I saw on the field with the
Huskers, only dialed back and more playful. I watched him
maneuver, being serious and trying to score, but also being
lighthearted and smiling the whole time.

Evan had a bright smile with white teeth. He was the sweetest, most thoughtful soul in the world, but he almost looked dangerous when he smiled. Maybe his smile was just dangerous for me. Never, in the history of the universe had someone been as attracted to a man as I was to Evan King. Never had someone loved a man as much as I loved him. I had wanted him since we were kids.

I watched him in awe, wondering how in the world I had ended up here. I thought about seeing him on the beach after his brother passed away. If that wouldn't have happened, he wouldn't have noticed my smell when we ran into each other in Corpus Christi. Then maybe he wouldn't have come to seek me out. I thought of all the unlikely events that had to happen in order for us to get to this place. I thought of all the potential partners we had both met in the years when we lost contact.

I sat there, watching Evan and his family, and I took in the situation for the miracle it was. It was almost too good to be true.

It is too good to be true, I reminded myself. I had a life and a whole career in a whole different city—one I had worked extremely hard for. But I watched Evan and his family, feeling little to no remorse about the fact that I wanted to abandon everything and move home to Galveston.

What would I even do here? I had a couple of connections in Houston, but nothing that could get me an instant job. I'd be starting over, and it would be an hour-long commute from

Galveston to Houston every day, anyway. At least that, with traffic.

I would have these urgent thoughts, and then I would tell myself to slow down—that there was no rush.

And then I would watch Evan some more and remember that I was very much in a rush.

I carried on a conversation with Evan's mom and Ms. Laney, but I watched the game the whole time. They played for over an hour. There were two teams of seven at first, and then it started to dwindle after about an hour when the older guys, Daniel and James, quit playing and came to the porch to talk to us. Some others followed a little while later, and finally, as another hour passed, there were just a few guys left out there—Evan, Will, Trey, Jacob, and of course, Mac and Theo.

A few people had to leave, and others shifted around the house, doing other things. I stayed on the porch the whole time. Abby and Laney got up after a while, but there was usually someone out there with me. They were all really friendly and welcoming.

"All right, let's finish this drive, and we're done," Evan said, finally.

"Awww, mannn!" Mac said, kicking the ground.

Evan nudged his chin at Mac. "Hey, dude, where are your manners?"

"Thank you," Mac said in a humbled but rushed tone, shaping up as he got into position on the line of scrimmage.

I watched as they finished that play and a few more.

And then the game was over, and they all slapped hands and patted each other like guys do when they finish a sporting event.

I had been sitting in a rocking chair, but I stood up and walked to the edge of the porch when I saw that Evan was headed toward me.

"We'll eat dinner in a little while," Abby announced opening the door.

"Hey," I heard Evan say, getting my attention.

I turned to find that he was looking at me. He held up his arms like he wanted me to come to him. I smiled and felt like I was floating on air. I hardly remembered walking down the steps to meet him at the bottom. He smiled and took me lightly into his arms, resting his hand on my back.

"I'm sweaty," he said. He was slightly sweaty, but I honestly didn't mind it. I wanted to kiss the damp place on his temple, just to taste the salt of his sweat. *Oh, gosh, what was the matter with me? Kissing sweat? Yes, actually. On Evan? Yes.* I felt all sorts of warm, gushy feelings in the deepest parts of my body.

"You played two hours of backyard ball," I said to him. "I'd be more surprised if you *weren't* sweaty."

He leaned down and kissed me unashamedly, gloriously pressing his mouth to mine. He tasted like salt from sweat, and his lips came against mine with a stamping force he had never used with me before. He wasn't being rough with me, but it was nowhere near as gentle as other kisses he had given me. The pressure of it combined with the taste of his mouth... I was... I couldn't...

"Ohh," I said helplessly when he pulled back.

He laughed at me for that. He had his hand on my back as he looked down at me. People were still gathered on the porch, but nobody seemed to care what we were doing. The pressure of Evan's grip intensified as he drew me close. He leaned in to whisper to me.

"Iz-zy," he said, his voice husky and low.

"At your service," I said, leaning close to him.

I was still reeling from that kiss—thinking about him doing it right there where his family could see.

"Let's me and you be late for dinner," he said.

"Okay," I agreed even though I had no idea what he was talking about. I didn't care. I was agreeing to whatever he was proposing.

"Let's go to the beach," he said.

"I can't get my cast wet, but..."

"I'm not trying to swim," he said. "Although that would be really fun. I wasn't thinking we'd do that tonight. I thought we'd just go walking or whatever—anything. Just get away. I need to be alone with youuu," he added, trailing off in a stiff, hoarse whisper.

"I knowww," I whispered back with a bit of the same urgent whisper he was using.

"Let's do it. Let's go to the beach. Hey, Izzy and I will be back for dinner," Evan announced to the people on the porch. He knew we might have passengers if he said we were going to the beach, so he didn't specify where we were going.

"I'll tell your mom," Laney said. "We might be gone when you get back," she added. "But we're so happy you're home, Evan, and it was good seeing you, Izzy."

"Yes, ma'am, it was good seeing you, too. Tell your husband and Jenny and Josh I said 'bye' if you guys end up leaving."

"Will do, sweetheart. You have a good trip back home."

"Thank you," I said, smiling, even though I didn't want to think about going home.

Evan told his aunt goodbye and we decided to go in the house to announce our departure to the rest of them since we already knew we weren't coming back right away.

"Where are you going?" Mac asked, even though he was spending the night at Nana and Pap's and would definitely see us when we got back.

"None-ya," Evan said.

"Do you know what that means, Theo?" Daniel asked, hearing Evan say the phrase.

Theo shook his head.

"None of your business," Daniel said.

"I told Izzy I'd take her to… we're just going out for a minute. We'll be back for dinner, probably," Evan said, explaining to Mac.

"Don't rush," Lucy said.

And within a couple of minutes, we were in Evan's truck.

He started the ignition and turned on the radio and the air conditioner. I smiled at the sounds of the Beastie Boys, which was what the boys wanted to listen to on the way there.

Evan turned it down. He reached out and pressed the button to eject the disk, and he put something else in.

"What is it?" I asked.

"Taj Mahal," he said.

"Did I tell you I went and bought one of his records after you recommended him?"

"You did," he said.

"Yeah, he's good. The guy at the record store told me about Dr. John when I bought that Taj Mahal album, and I liked him, too. Did I tell you this already?"

"You did, and neither time did I love it when you talked about the guy at the record store. Who is this record store clown anyway? I never really talk to anybody when I go to a record store."

Evan was joking around. He wasn't really mad, but he was acting like it, and I loved it.

"I got clowns to the left of me and jokers to the right," I said, acting annoyed and quoting the lyrics of the popular song.

"You better not," he said.

I smiled at him and leaned toward him as he drove. "I'm just talking about the song," I said.

"Yeah, but old Tommy Timmons on the news station is drooling all over you."

"Tommy Timmons, who's that?"

"Shane Henderson."

"Lance?" I asked.

"Yes," he said. "Whatever his name is. And now this dirtbag at the record store."

He was being funny, I knew it by the way he talked, and I laughed and took his hand, holding it. I pulled it to my chest, cradling him against me and feeling a surge of electricity at the places where his skin touched mine.

"It's the first time I really get to see you alone and enjoy it. It's our first time in a long time." I took a slow, deep breath. "I was missing you," I added, speaking softly to him. I didn't mean to sound vulnerable, but I was vulnerable.

He gripped my hand. He kept his eyes on the road, but he held onto me and I held onto him.

"Izzy, I hate tomorrow."

"Don't say it," I said, instinctually.

"Don't go then."

I let out a breath. "I know, Evan. I know." I wanted to cry. I desperately wanted to stay with him. "Let's think about how I can make the transition from Corpus Christi," I said. "I'll take a few months and figure out what to do about work. I'll wrap up things there and start thinking about options here."

"Really?" he asked, hopefully.

"Yes," I said. "Of course. I'd much rather have you than my job. I can find work to do here. To me, work is second place to being near you."

"Thank you," he said in a relieved tone. "Because I feel the same way. I assumed I'd be here because of the store, but now I'm thinking about how I can open a location in Corpus."

"No, I know you were looking forward to being near your family," I said.

He brought my hand to his mouth. "But just know that it's not all on you to make the move," he said. "If we need to be in Corpus Christi for now for your job, I can make that happen."

"No, no, it makes more sense with both of us having family here and everything. Plus, I know you have plans with the store, and you like your uncle's gym. We'll work it out. I'll come here. It's no problem. It might take a little while to make the transition, but I'm up for coming here with you. And in the meantime, while I'm getting things settled, we can try to see each other as many weekends as possible. Four hours is a piece of cake compared to Nebraska."

CHAPTER 18

*C*orpus Christi was a larger city than Galveston. It had its own news station, and there were more professional opportunities for me there. On paper, Corpus Christi was the right choice. But, as we all know, love has nothing to do with paper.

There was just no question that I would move back home to Galveston. I was excited about it. I loved my home, and I couldn't wait to get back here and start a life with Evan.

It felt official now that we had a conversation about it. Evan and I decided to enjoy every moment we had together. I held onto him in the truck on the way to the beach, and we didn't break contact from there on out.

He parked at Bermuda Beach. It was late in the afternoon, and the weather was gorgeous. We left our shoes in his truck and set out for a walk, both of us in the best mood, laughing and being playful with each other.

"How are you feeling?" he asked.

"A-ma-zing," I said, referring to the fact that I was walking on the beach holding Evan King's hand. I leaned on his arm, feeling the dreamy ocean breeze and the sand between my toes. "Wonderful," I added, since *amazing* didn't seem like enough. "Perfect."

He laughed and shook his head, taking me into his arms and clutching me against his broad chest. We had been walking slowly, but he slowed and then stopped completely, turning me and pulling me into his arms.

"I meant how are you holding up," Evan said, holding me gently, checking me out, and giving me an irresistible, easy smile. "You've been out-and-about all day," he explained. Evan held me in his arms, but he pulled back just enough so that he could focus on my face. "How are your stitches?"

"Fine," I said. "I looked at them in the bathroom when we were at your mom's house, and they're fine."

"How about your head?"

"Evan, my head is fine. My head is in the clouds, I barely even know I have a head anymore."

"What's that mean? Are you feeling sick?" he asked, his face getting serious for a second.

I laughed. "No, I'm… I'm not. My head is in the clouds because of you. This. I feel like I'm lightning in a jar right now. Like I could just burst out of my own skin."

"I feel so much like I could burst out of my own skin, Izzy, you have no idea. It's taking all of my strength to keep from throwing you over my shoulder and running into the water with you. I want to do crazy things like that. I've been missing you so much that now that I have you, it's like I—"

"Don't know where to begin?"

"Yes."

I kissed him, I didn't ask for permission. I stretched upward, using a grip on his arms for leverage, and I kissed him. My mouth was dry, so I pulled back and licked my lips, smiling a little before kissing him again.

Evan needed no further encouragement. He caught me up, latching his big arms around me like a vice. His mouth came to mine, and it was with great expertise, and torturous gentleness that he teased me with his lips, teeth, tongue. He flexed his arms around me and deepened the kiss, and my blood turned to hot liquid. I was weak, soft, relaxed, given over to him. My body literally ached. The warm, silky rhythm was too much. I felt like I was on the edge of a cliff.

Only I wasn't scared of falling.

I felt more like I might explode into a million bits of glitter as I went off the edge.

Evan stood on the beach and claimed me with that kiss. Nothing else existed besides us in that moment. Evan kissed me deeply, drawing me to the edge of that precipice before pulling back and kissing me lightly again. He was relentless. He loved me and he wanted me, and he told me those things, plain as day but without words during that kiss.

I broke the kiss after what must have been five full minutes. Maybe it was ten. Who cared? My Evan, my wonderful Evan. He was funny and kind, and Hollywood-leading-man-handsome with his playful smile and his eyes, the dark blue color of stormy waters. He flashed his white teeth at me.

"You, Izzy," he said.

"Me what?" I asked.

"You... are... mine..." He said the words slowly and shook his head dazedly, staring at me with a dangerous gleam in his eye.

"I *am* yours," I promised.

I looked to the side and discreetly cleared my throat before blinking up at him again. I made a certain familiar, professional curious expression and got into a softer version of my newscaster's voice. "We're here with Evan King, Evan, let me ask, what will you do with me, now that I'm yours."

My stage voice and demeanor were similar to the way I acted in real life, but they were different enough that I knew it was surreal for him to hear me switch modes.

Evan smiled and licked his lips in a nervous but still extremely attractive motion. "I will do... *everything* with you," he said. "That's the point of being mine. You're my everything now. My date to a wedding, you. My movies on Friday night, you. With me at Christmas, you. *Everything* is what I'm going to do with you." He lowered his mouth to my ear. I felt the warm skin of his cheek against my ear. "Eve-ry-thing," he whispered.

It was a dare. His voice was low and velvety, and I wanted to melt simply from the sound of it.

And then I realized what he was implying, and I swooned. It was a fake one, but I made it dramatic, where I put the backside of my hand to my head and wilted slowly, swaying with a light helpless breathy whimper like you picture in a romance novel. Evan knew what I was doing, and he laughed as he caught me in his arms, saving me from falling. I smiled as I straightened again.

"I *love* you," he said smiling. He said it with emphasis on the word love, which struck me as funny.

"I *love* you too," I said, matching his style.

He stared at my mouth, smirked, and licked his lips before kissing me again. I tasted the faintest hint of salt, from his sweat, or from the sea, or maybe both. It was perfect and it caused me to feel the swoony, melty feelings that I had been pretending to have a moment before.

I leaned up and kissed his neck. I was tucked in so close that no one could see me do it. I definitely tasted salt when I did that, and I smiled and leaned up to do it again.

"Izzy, uhhhh," he trailed off in a hoarse groan when I kissed his neck again, my mouth partially open this time.

He pulled me closer with his hand around my back. I could feel the pulse in his neck, and the speed of it, made me have warm, rushing, expectant feelings.

"Oh my gosh, Izzy, I have to stop this before I put you in my truck and drive all the way to Las Vegas."

Evan moved, kissing me, clutching me to him like an insatiable beast. I laughed and wiggled before adjusting and holding him back.

He stopped moving and settled me into his arms again. This moment was the stuff of dreams—the movement, the feel of our bodies shifting and touching in the late afternoon wind—the waves, the sand, Evan. Gosh, Evan. I swayed in his arms feeling like there was music in the air.

"Evan King!"

We heard people calling his name, and we turned to find a group of people, two guys and two girls—all were approximately our age. I should have known Evan would get recognized. As they got closer, I recognized them, also. They were Evan's age, people we had gone to high school with.

"Whoa, is that Izzy Abbott?" a guy asked.

It was Craig Gilbert who asked, and I smiled and waved at him.

"It is," I said. "How are you, Craig?" I turned to face them more fully as they approached us. I was going to step away from Evan, but he held me close. I glanced at him, and he smiled confidently at me.

"What happened to your arm?" Mandy Pinkerton asked.

But at the same time her sister Jeanne said, "Are you two dating now?"

Also, at the same time, Craig asked Evan something about football.

It was a chaotic few seconds, and I answered Mandy since she was the loudest and closest to me. "I got in a car accident a couple of days ago."

Evan answered Craig, saying something about recently moving back from Nebraska.

There was a minute of this type of chaotic small talk where we talked over each other, and then Mandy said, "So, I guess you two are together."

It was during a moment when conversation was quiet, so everyone looked at Evan and me.

"Yeah," Evan said easily. "We're getting married."

"You're kidding, when?" Mandy asked. "I didn't even know you were dating," she added.

Evan was popular in Galveston, and if he got engaged, people would mention it.

"Soon," he said. "I just got back, and Izzy is still in Corpus Christi. She does a news show down there."

"Oh, really?" Craig said.

"I heard you were doing that," Mandy said.

We talked for a few more minutes before Evan told them we needed to be going.

He and I held hands, staying connected on the way back to the truck, and then on the way back to his parents' house.

We took the long way, stopping to walk down Bank Street so he could take me by the hardware store. It was closed, but Evan had a key and I wanted to go by there for old time's sake.

We both realized that the stop at the hardware store was just an excuse to have a few more minutes alone. I was glad we stopped, though. I loved the smell in that store. It was vintage and nostalgic.

We went to eat at his parents' house after our brief stop on Bank Street. Most of his family had left by the time we got back, but Laney was still there with Jenny. Lucy, Mac, and Theo were there, too, obviously, since they were spending the night.

I stayed with him until 10pm that evening. We knew that when Evan took me home that night, I wouldn't see him again for two weeks.

My dad and I would leave in the morning bright and early for Corpus Christi. I had a charity benefit to attend this weekend, and Evan had already made a commitment to speak to the youth group. Neither of us could make the trip this coming weekend, so we knew it might end up being two weeks.

"I'm desperate, Izzy," he said, when he pulled into my parents' driveway.

"I'm desperate, too," I said.

"What do we do?" he asked.

He put the truck in park and turned off his lights.

"I don't know, Evan. I guess we have to wait two weeks."

"I feel bad about it," he said in a desperate tone. "I might come during the week even though you're working. Are you sure you can go back to work? Are you sure you feel up for it?"

"I'll be fine," I assured him since I could tell he was worried about me.

I leaned into Evan, feeling exhausted after a long day, but also desperately dreading leaving him.

In spite of the late hour, my mom came outside to talk to Evan and thank him for all he did at the hospital. She had missed him when he came over yesterday and we were rushed this morning, so I wasn't surprised that she came outside to catch him.

Her appearance threw me off just enough that I didn't cry when Evan left. Her showing up during our goodbye was awkward, but I was thankful for the distraction so that I wasn't a blubbering idiot for his departure. It was already hard enough as it was. I held back tears as we promised to see each other as soon as possible and to be in touch every day on the phone.

CHAPTER 19

I fell asleep feeling elated and heartbroken in portions that were so equal it was surreal, dizzying.

I had trouble getting to sleep and trouble staying that way. I woke up sweaty several times during the night.

I dreamed a lot, and I woke up restless and agitated with my heart racing.

My dream during the morning hours was the worst. I dreamed about another car accident, but this time it was Evan who had gotten into it. It was Evan in the car instead of me.

I was flustered and upset about the dream when I woke up, but I reasoned with myself over a 6am cup of coffee, and I managed to see the dream for a positive and not a negative.

I knew I dreamed my fears sometimes, and I knew I dreamed about losing Evan because losing him was something I was very afraid of.

I had worked tirelessly for years to get to the place where I was professionally, yet losing that would be much easier than losing Evan. It must have been God who helped me see it. I felt a certain type of peace that just settled over me, neutralizing my nervous, fretful thoughts and turning them into thoughts that were logical, orderly, calm.

That feeling of losing Evan in the dream made me understand how important it was for me to be with him.

I couldn't put it off.

We had already spent too much time apart.

It was time for that to be over.

There was a phrase, *live like there's no tomorrow*, and I knew that was what I had to do.

I truly understood that phrase now.

Living apart from Evan was no longer an option for me. I had to make the most of every single moment on this earth. I couldn't lose any more time.

My father came into the kitchen at 7am.

"Oh, you're up already? Mom thought she heard the coffee pot, but we both thought you'd sleep in after staying out all day yesterday." He walked across the kitchen and whistled a quick tune before he continued speaking. "I figured we'd get on the road first thing. I'll want to help you get situated with a rental car and everything before I come back."

"I'm not going," I said.

I spoke calmly because I had already had time to make the decision and sort through my feelings about it.

Dad's gaze shot to me, and I took in his worried expression. "Are you okay?" he asked, thinking I couldn't make the trip.

"Yes, sir. I'm fine. I'm wonderful, actually."

"What's that mean?"

"I had a nightmare last night."

"Now I'm really confused," he said.

I smiled as I stood from the barstool that I'd been sitting on for the last hour.

"The dream just made me realize that I was afraid of something, and then I figured out that it was something I had control of, so I'm taking control of it."

"What is it?"

"Evan."

"Evan King?"

"Of course, Dad."

"What about him?"

"I'm staying with him," I said. "I was planning on going home and taking months to quit my job and sell my house and make the transition back here, but I'm—"

"Wait. You're selling your house?"

"Yes sir."

"Are you moving here?"

"Yes. Today. I live here now. Officially. That's what I'm telling you. I'm not going back to Corpus Christi. I'll have to make trips, obviously, to get my things, and pack, and meet with realtors, but I'm not going today. Maybe I'll go back for that event this weekend. I need to talk to Evan."

I paused and stared at my dad with a little smile.

"I assume you and Mom won't mind if I stay here for a little while before I get my own place."

"No, Izabel, but what about your job?"

"It's just a job. I'm replaceable," I said. "If I would have died in that car accident the other night, they would have had to—"

"Don't say that, Izabel," Mom said, coming into the room and hearing me say that last part.

"Izabel's talking about not going home to Corpus Christi," my father said.

"I'm not just talking about it," I said. "I've decided. I'm not going back—not to live, at least. If you don't mind, I'll stay here for a little while so I can get my housing situation squared away. I'll probably buy something here and roll the equity from one house to the other."

My mom crossed the room as I was speaking, and the whole time she walked toward me, she was staring at me with a completely confused expression.

"What's the matter?" I asked, based on her expression.

"Slow down," she said. "What's going on, now?"

"I came in here to Izabel telling me she didn't want to make the trip to Corpus Christi today."

"I don't," I agreed easily.

"You can't do that," Mom said, blinking at me.

I started to speak and defend myself, but I hesitated, reminding myself that they needed time to let this decision process. "I *can* do this," I said, trying to sound as humble as possible. "That's the whole thing. It's my choice to make. I mean, the part about staying with you and dad for a while, that's a choice you have to make, but I—"

"Of course we want you to stay here with us, Izzy, but baby, think about this for a second. Are you saying you want to think about not going back to your job?"

"Yes, ma'am," I said.

"Why would you do that?" Mom asked.

I took a deep breath. "The short answer is that I've fallen in love. But there are other things, too—you guys, my family, his family, the hardware store, the gym, Galveston in general."

"Izabel, you've worked for years for that job. You must know what a shock it is to hear you say you don't want to—"

"I know, Mama. I know all that. But you know what? I'm soooo relieved now that I made this decision. I don't want to go back."

"No offense, honey, because I know you're grown and you know what you're doing, but it just feels a little sudden. You know, you and Evan are… wh, what did he say about it? Did he say he wanted you to quit your job?"

"No, he didn't. I mean, yeah, he knows I wanted to eventually… he doesn't know I'm staying today. He thinks I'm heading back to Corpus Christi this morning with dad. We're supposed to see each other in two weeks."

"And that's too long?" my mom asked, still confused.

I paused for a moment. "Yes," I said simply. "Evan would come to me if I asked him. If he knew I was making this decision, he would offer to come over there with me." I shrugged resolutely, looking at my mom. "But I, one hundred percent, want to stay, here. Now that I've decided to do this, I realized how happy it'll make me. I don't care about my job. If anything, that job was just to get me to that hotel so I could run into Evan there. I'll find something to do here. I'll figure something out with the station in Houston, or I can help Evan with the hardware store. I'm not worried about a job. I'll figure that part out. I'm just excited about being back home. I've been sitting here, working it all out in my mind, and I feel nothing but relief about it. The station will be fine without me. Ginger Riddle will be thrilled to have her segment back. That's what I was saying to dad, if things have been different in a car accident, they would have to replace me, anyway."

My mom came up to me and hugged me. "Well, I don't like you talking like that, but gosh honey, we would be so excited to have you back home." She squeezed me gently. "So excited," she added. She breathed deep. "We'll figure it out," she said, talking to Dad as she broke the hug with me.

"She's not the first person to quit a job," Dad said. "Not even the first one at that news station."

"Thanks, Dad," I said. I was thankful for his kind reassurance, but honestly, I didn't need it. I didn't feel remorse. The reluctance my parents had at first didn't sway me a bit. I was staying in Galveston. My decision to stay brought along all sorts of feelings of peace, joy, and excitement.

"In a minute, I'm going to call and talk to my producer," I said. "I have a friend in real estate, too, and I'll probably give her a call. I'm going to have some business to take care of on the phone. It'll be long distance, and I'll just pay you guys back."

"Don't worry about things like that," my mom said. "Just take care of your business. But maybe make sure Evan wants you to do this, though, before you go making all these..."

I smiled at her and shook my head, and she trailed off. She didn't mean to offend me. I could have explained, validated us, but I didn't feel that it was necessary. "Evan's going to love this," I assured her, smiling as I walked down the hall to make my phone calls.

CHAPTER 20

I was nervous, but I wasn't scared. I had butterflies, but they weren't the reluctant ones. I made phone calls and set things in motion.

I told my producer the truth—that the car accident had changed my life and that I was moving home. She and I had always had a good relationship, and we talked for an hour. I was candid with her, and on a human level, she understood.

She was kind about it and gave her best wishes. I told her I was still planning on showing up at the event and that I would see her this weekend.

I called my realtor friend and set up a meeting for Saturday, the morning of the charity event. It felt so good to just rip the band-aid off and start making moves.

I got dressed after I made a few phone calls. I took my time showering and drying my hair and putting on just enough makeup to feel confident and comfortable.

It was nine-thirty by the time I left the house. I hadn't driven a car since my accident, and I wondered if I would be okay, but I was so preoccupied with the other events in my life that I didn't think much about the mechanics of driving or whether or not I was mentally okay with it. I just said goodbye to my parents and got into my father's truck. I was focused on Evan, and I drove without contemplating it.

I went straight to the hardware store. I figured if he was there, I could surprise him, and if he wasn't, they'd tell me where I could find him. I liked the idea of seeing him at the hardware store, though. I thought it would be a nice place to surprise him.

My heart was pounding by the time I got to Bank Street. I felt calm and happy with my decision, but I was overwhelmed with thoughts of telling Evan and wondering how the scene would play out.

I imagined several different scenarios and most of them included finding him on an aisle and saying 'excuse me, sir', or tapping him on the shoulder when he was looking the other way. I hoped I was able to catch him there.

Oh, yep, and there was his truck.

As soon as I saw it parked on Bank Street, my whole body came alive with anticipation. I had to hold back the gigantic smile that threatened to cover my face. I parked, got out of my dad's truck, and walked to the hardware store.

I felt like I could hear piano music playing in the soundtrack of my life as I peered down the first aisle, expecting to find Evan there.

"Hey, let me know if you need any help," I heard a woman say from behind me.

I turned, expecting to find Evan's mother or grandmother, but it was a young woman who I didn't recognize.

She was cute. She had a ponytail and a t-shirt that said King's Hardware right across the chest. I felt a stab of jealousy. I was jealous over that t-shirt, of all things. I needed one of those. I was thrown off, and it didn't help that she was pretty. I tried to see if I could recognize her, but I didn't.

"Thank you," I said.

If I couldn't find Evan within a minute, I would ask someone for help, but for now, I would try to find him on my own.

My search lasted all of five minutes and then I located a different store employee, an older man, and asked him if he happened to know where Evan was.

"I think he's in the back," he said. "Would you like me to see if I can get him for you?"

"Uh, um, ye-yes sir, but, uh, w-would it be possible for me to just... go with you instead of... I was going to try to surprise Evan, and—"

I stopped talking when the man put a hand on my shoulder. "Of course, sweetie, I'll take you back there, and we'll see if we can find Evan together. Come on back here with me."

I smiled as I followed the man. He had on a polo shirt with the smaller King's Hardware logo embroidered on one side of his chest. I noticed his shirt as we were taking off toward the back of the store, and out of nervousness, I mentioned it as we walked.

"I like your shirt. I like the t-shirt version... I saw another girl with a t-shirt on. Those are cool."

"Oh, our work shirts?"

"Yes, sir," I said, pausing awkwardly and wondering how I somehow went from professional conversationalist to someone who was literally unable to think of something to say.

"How do you know Evan?" he asked.

"I'm his... I'm his girl." I didn't want to call myself his girlfriend so I just left it at *I'm his girl*. "He's my man," I added, as if that clarified.

"Oh, really? Well, nice to meet you, I'm Randall. I've been knowing Evan since before he was born."

"Yes sir. I remember the name Mister Randall. I grew up here and I went to school with Evan and Phillip and Lucy. My name is Izzy Abbott."

"Huh, Tim and Dot Abbott?"

"They're my grandparents, on my dad's side, yes sir."

"Okay, so your dad is..."

"Mark."

Randall nodded as he opened the door that led to the hallway in the back of the hardware store. It seemed like I had been down there once before when I was little and needed to use the restroom.

"I know the Abbotts from State Farm," Randall said.

"Yes sir, my grandfather and uncle."

"Okay, well, it's nice to meet you. Mark Abbott's daughter."

He stopped walking when we reached the door that led to the loading dock and the alley.

"What'd you say your name was?"

"Izzy," I said. He opened the door and I came into the doorway as I said my name. There was a bay with two company vans and a group of guys were standing at the end of one of the vans. They looked our way when they noticed us in the doorway.

It was Evan's dad and two other guys, but my eyes just jumped from man to man, looking for Evan. My heart was pounding, expecting one of them to be Evan, but I didn't see him.

Finally, I saw a head peek out from the back of the van. I knew it was Evan and I was smiling by the time he turned to me.

I waved and watched him begin to move. His face was serious, concerned, and he climbed from the back of the van, jumping down with a spring in his step as he rounded the corner. I was at the top of a set of five or six steps, and Evan came around the van and the men who were standing there. I watched him take a few long strides, and just like that, he was at the bottom of the steps, looking up at me expectantly.

He paused briefly. "Are you okay?"

I nodded and smiled, and one second later, he scaled the steps and was standing right below me—basically on top of me.

Randall mumbled something about "Letting you two catch up," as he turned and walked back into the store.

Evan took me by the hand and took off walking with me so fast that I didn't even have time to think. He opened the door that Randall had just gone through. "Hey Mister Randall, this is my future wife right here. Izzy."

"Yes, sir, we met," Randall said.

He was still talking when Evan stopped and opened a door, pulling me into a... well, it was a closet.

It was dark in there except for the little light that came in through the slits in the vented door. It was cramped, too, a pantry-type room with three walls that had shelves. There was just a tiny area for us to stand in the middle. There were basic supplies like paper products and boxes of sponges and trash bags. It was cramped in there, and I shook with laughter once he closed the door and we were in mostly darkness.

"What... are you laughing?" he asked.

"Yes," I said, still shaking with silent laughter.

"Are you okay?"

"Yes. I'm wondering why you shoved me in a supply closet."

"Because," Evan said, catching his breath.

"You said you were okay and nothing was wrong, and everyone was outside, and then I came in, and Randall... it just—this was the first place I could think of to get alone with you. What are you doing? I thought you weren't coming by before you left."

He leaned down, his mouth finding mine in the mostly dark closet. He pressed into me, kissing me. The closet forced us to be wonderfully close to each other, and Evan was leaning in, latching onto me like a big, wonderful ape.

I smiled and touched the side of his face, and he kissed me again. He held me close.

"Don't goooo," he begged in that same hoarse whisper. The sound of it caused my insides to turn into warm liquid.

"I'm not," I said, pulling him close. I kissed the warm skin of his neck. I was taking in the taste and feel of him and feeling overcome with happiness when Evan pulled back and looked at me.

He blinked.

Our eyes had adjusted by now, and the slats in the door provided plenty of light for me to make out his face. He stared fixedly at me.

"What do you mean you're not?"

"I'm not going back," I said. "I'll have to go back some time to get things and move and stuff, but I'm not going back today. I decided I live here now."

Evan crushed me with a kiss.

Excitement, and love, and passion, and happiness poured into me as Evan pulled me in and clamped his mouth to mine.

He moved, kissing me deeply and with so much fervor that I had to struggle to catch my breath when he broke the kiss. Both of us were breathing heavy. He took me into his arms, and we held each other passionately. The tightness in which we held each other showed just how relieved we both were.

Evan let out a groan. "Are you serious right now?" he asked.

"Yes. I called my producer and quit my job. I'm selling my place over there. I'm here now. I'm just going to stay with my parents until I—"

And there it was, another crushing kiss.

Evan kissed me deeply, finding an instant, deep, searching rhythm. I latched onto him, curling my toes and feeling like the pleasure might cause me to burst into pieces.

Evan showed me how happy he was by the way he kissed me. He kissed me deeply and then he broke the kiss, giving me two or three more soft, gentle, searching ones like he just couldn't stop. I loved the taste of him, and I smiled as he pulled away. He held my face in his hands and stared at me intensely.

"Thank you, Izzy, but you don't have to do this. I'll go to you. I'll move. I was already thinking about it. I was planning on coming to you and saying these same things. I'll move to Corpus Christi if you want me to. I only want to be with you."

"I only want to be with you, too," I said. "I'm fine. I'm happy. I want to come to Galveston. I already decided to come here. I talked to the station and a realtor already. I live here now. I have to go back some, obviously, to pack and take care of things, but I'm—"

He kissed me again. And then he ducked smelling me and hugging me and holding me—moving, touching me. He kissed my cheek, rubbing his cheek gently against mine. I felt wetness on his cheek, and I pulled back as I reached up to touch his cheek. There were tears streaming down his face, and I pulled him near, feeling absolutely wrecked with emotion.

"I love you," he whispered.

"I love you, too," I said.

"Let's get a house and married and stuff," he said.

I couldn't hold back a little laugh. "Either that, or I'm buying one of my own, because I don't know how long I can share a bedroom with my mom's exercise room. She's on that treadmill at 7am."

"Let's just rent something for a year or two," Evan said. "That way we can work out our income and see what's what. Then we'll buy or build."

We were in the privacy of the dark closet, so Evan just paused what he was saying every ten seconds or so to kiss me. The last one was open-mouthed. He was insatiable. We had to get married.

"We have to get married," I said when the thought crossed my mind.

"Yes. Now. When? Should we seriously go elope? When can we do this?"

I was laughing because I could tell he was in a hurry. He was moving, kissing my neck, face, or mouth anytime he wasn't talking. We were in a supply closet, and it felt more like heaven.

Evan wrapped his big, muscular body around me, holding me. I let out a little whimper at the pleasure of it all.

The nearby door opened, and we heard voices of the men who were coming inside. Evan held onto the inside handle, just in case someone decided to pull it.

The group walked by, talking and laughing, and after a second, I realized they were talking about Evan.

"I give him a year," someone said.

"To what?"

"To get married."

My eyes widened, and Evan put his finger to my mouth, telling me to be quiet.

"I give him less than that," another man said.

"He told his mom he would move to Corpus Christi if he had to."

"Move? He just g-got home!"

"Well, we'll have to see what happens with him and this Abbott girl."

Their voices had gotten farther away as they spoke. I could tell they walked right by the closet. Evan let go of the handle and moved to hold me again.

"Marry me, my love." He kissed me over and over again on the neck, smelling me, and kissing me relentlessly.

"Yes," I said. "Pleeease."

Evan gave me a mischievous grin and I put my hand to his face.

"This is my favorite minute I've ever had," I said.

He looked at me with that gorgeous, easy smile. "We're in a broom closet," he said. He kissed me again.

"Is that where we are?" I asked breathlessly.

EPILOGUE

Six months later

*E*van and I got married right away. We rented an
apartment in a building Tara and Trey owned, and we
had now been there for about five months.

I had no regrets whatsoever about leaving Corpus Christi
to come home and start a life with Evan. I was happy doing
exactly what I was doing.

I had a plan in the works for something I could do with
a news station. It was a meet your neighbor segment, and it
would only air in Galveston. A few Houston stations reported
Galveston news, but none of them had a specific Galveston
segment.

I could use a cameraman and editor to film once a week.
I could do five or six interviews in one day. I had worked at a
news station and I knew it would be worth it for them to send
a small crew down once a week. Tara and Trey had an office
space for lease that would do the trick for a location. I could

also be a correspondent covering some live events in Galveston when they needed me to.

I was trying to have the best of both worlds where I didn't have to leave Galveston or go to work every day. It was a very specific job that I made up for myself. I knew my chances were slim, but I didn't want to work too much. I loved my life as it was, and I would sooner not work at all than work too much.

As it stood, I was able to help Evan with his ideas for the hardware store. He proposed a new distribution system where he would set up a sales team and reps would work with contractors. The reps would manage direct wholesale ordering through the store.

Evan and Will would work for a salary plus a minimal percentage of total sales. This only pushed them to make the whole operation a success. They worked hard on it, and I liked to help. I was busy with that, and a news show would have to fit with my schedule.

But that being said... I really wanted to do it. I missed conducting interviews. I missed getting dressed up and sitting up straight and asking people questions. I liked feeling like I could help folks learn something interesting about each other—I had fun doing that.

I was working on the package I would send to the producers at three different Houston area stations. I had footage of me from Corpus Christi, and I combined it with footage I had taken in Galveston during the last month with help from Evan and Will.

I had done interviews with five locals, including Aunt Tess and Uncle Billy. I made a little art project to send with my package as a personal touch. It was a pop-up card—a cut-out image of myself in a chair, leaning to one side, like I was interviewing someone. On the card, I explained my hopes and goals for the segment and said that I would love to hear from them.

In an ideal world, all of the stations would want me and we would have a bidding war to see who I go to.

But the most likely scenario was that no one or maybe just one of them would call.

If someone called, I hoped it was Channel 13, but all I could do was show them what I had to offer and wait to see if I was a good fit for any of them.

Evan had been at the store all afternoon, and when he got home, I was knee-deep in paper and glue as I worked on the pop-up cards.

"Hey," I said when he came into the living room. "I didn't even hear you come in."

"That's because you're blaring Al Green in here."

He was smiling as he came up to me, and I unfolded my legs and stood up from my mess at the coffee table so that I could greet him. Evan smiled as he leaned in to kiss me. I was lightheaded from standing so fast... or maybe it was just Evan who made me feel that way. I leaned into him, and his mouth came to mine, sticking to it in a lazy kiss.

"How was your afternoon?" I asked feeling warm and fuzzy after he kissed me.

"I just talked to Lucy," he said.

Evan let me go and leaned down to pick up one of the little cards I was working on. I had made three of them, and he grabbed the one that was closest to the edge.

"I didn't know Lucy was in town," I said.

"Yeah. She came in this morning to have lunch with Mom. Will brought your videos by the store, and we watched it."

"Oh, really? Will didn't tell me he was done. Where are they?"

I glanced around, looking for them. Will had a friend with some audio/video equipment, and he had edited the audition videos for me to send to the stations.

"Well, in all the excitement, I left them at the store."

"In what excitement?"

"Lucy *loved* it," he said, walking to the other side of the room. He grabbed the phone off of the charger and dialed a number.

"She loved the video?" I asked.

"I'll let her tell you," Evan said, nodding with the phone to his ear. "Hey, I just got home, I have Izzy right here. I'm gonna let you talk to her. Hang on."

Evan handed me the phone and I put it to my ear, looking at him with a puzzled expression that made him smile at me.

He widened his dark blue eyes and gestured for me to go ahead and talk.

"Hello?" I said.

"Hey, Izzy."

"Hey, Lucy."

"Hey, I saw your video. That was amazing. You're so good."

"Aw, thank you! I'm glad they came out good. I actually haven't seen it yet."

When I said that to Lucy, I shrugged curiously at Evan as if asking where they were, and he gestured for me to pay attention to the conversation.

"Oh, it came out amazing. I actually saw it earlier today when Will first brought it by the store. I asked him if I could have a copy. I was on my way to lunch, but then I knew my father-in-law was in town, so I took it by his house. He watched it, Izzy, and he agreed with me! So, he called a friend and he's setting up a meeting with somebody over at one of the news stations. He said they'd flip over you!"

My heart was racing. I didn't want to get my hopes up, but it certainly sounded like good news. But then I remembered that the video said nothing of the boundaries I had already decided on.

"Thank you so much," I said, trying not to sound worried when it was technically good news. "The only thing is that I had this whole card explaining that I don't live in Houston and couldn't work full time. I was going to put it in with—"

"Evan told me," Lucy said, cutting me off. "I know you're not looking for anything full-time. I told my father-in-law you have your own terms and want to work in Galveston."

"What did he say?"

"He said you could probably name your terms and price and everything with how good you were. He works with those people all the time, and he said you could be on the national news."

I wanted to squeal, but I held it inside. I did do a little dance, trying to be quiet, and Evan came up to me, pulling me into his arms.

"Seriously, Izzy. Evan said you were making packages, but you don't need to send those in," she said. "I left the video with the Senator, and he told me he'd get it to the right person. He said to just wait for a phone call."

"Oh, my gosh, Lucy. I don't even know what to say. Thank you. Thank you so much for doing that."

"It's my pleasure," she said. "I'm proud of you. Those came out really good. I had never heard that story about Uncle Billy finding that hundred dollar bill when he was a kid."

"Yeah, that was interesting. He told me he hadn't told many people that story."

"That's what I'm saying," Lucy said. "You did a good job. Those interviews were fun and interesting."

"Thank you. Your aunt and uncle were probably being nice, too, trying to give me something interesting and new."

"It doesn't matter what made them do it. What matters is the fact is you're the interviewer that made it happen. I've seen them both get interviewed before, and they're good, but with you, it was just... I don't know, more transparent. It was endearing. Fun to watch. You really do a great job."

"Thank you," I said, feeling humbled by the compliment.

"All right, well, I'm taking off for Houston so I can make it back for Mac's football game. But I'm glad Evan caught me in time to tell you the good news... Drew's dad said not to send your thing in. He's got the video, and he's going to take care of it."

"Wow," I said, stunned. "Thanks, Lucy. Thank you for doing that."

"Oh, I'm happy to. I'm proud of you. You should have heard the senator. *You mean I'm related to this young woman?*" Her voice came across the phone and a deep, gruff tone as she imitated her father-in-law.

I laughed. "Did he say that?"

"Yes!" she said, laughing. "He was all proud. He said he's going to get you to interview him sometime."

"I, I don't know how to repay you."

"You could talk my brother into coming to Mac's game tonight. They're playing a little team right here in Pearland, so it's not far for y'all. It starts at six-thirty. Mac would be ecstatic if I could talk Uncle Evan into coming."

"I'll talk to Evan, but that seems like a possibility."

"Okay, I'll leave the address here at Mom's. If you decide to come, just call and get it from her."

"Sounds good," I said.

I hung up with Lucy and stared at Evan. He was already close to me, but he pulled me into his arms once I dropped the phone.

"Your presence is requested at a football game in Pearland," I said. "And I vote for going," I added. "I could go for a Frito Chili Pie for dinner."

Evan smiled, nestling his face into my neck like he often did. My husband loved the way I smelled. He was always hugging on me, smelling my neck. I loved it that he did that and, in the morning, I would put on something that smelled good, knowing that he would come up to hug me sometime during the day.

He kissed my neck and then pulled back to stare at me. "Mac's game? Is it tonight?"

"Yeah," I said. "I think it'd be fun. We haven't been to the last few, and I was planning on working, but it seems like I don't need to finish these cards."

He shook his head. "Can you believe that? Lucy was there meeting Mom when Will brought the tape, and she did the rest. It wasn't like I even asked her to show it to Drew's dad."

"I'm so excited," I said. "I'll get changed for the game."

"Don't," Evan said. He pulled back and stared at my chest. It was a t-shirt from the hardware store. It said King's Hardware in big letters across my chest—the same one that Samantha had on that day in the store. "I like seeing my name right there."

"It's my name, too, you big oaf."

But Evan knew what I meant by oaf. I was referring to the good, irresistible kind of oaf—the kind that ravished ladies and the ladies didn't mind. Evan leaned down and picked me up, and I yelped in surprise.

I wrapped my arms around him when I saw that he wasn't putting me down right away and I shook my head and beamed at him for being such a caveman.

"What time's that game?" he asked, holding me.

"She said it started at six-thirty."

Evan looked at the clock and was quiet for a few seconds as he thought about the time. "That still gives us thirty minutes before we need to leave," he said.

"Yeah, it does, doesn't it?" I agreed, staring at him with a challenging smile.

We both knew what we were really talking about. We were newlyweds, after all. And it wouldn't be the end of the world if we were a few minutes late to the game.

The End
(till book 6)

Thanks for reading Feels Like Home.
Bank Street Stories is a multi-generational romance.
All nine books in the series are now available!

Thanks to my team ~ Chris, Coda, Jan,
Glenda, Yvette, and Pete